About the author

John Beverley is the pen name of an author who wishes to retain anonymity, for fear of reprisals, adverse commentary, social ostracism, and all manner of other unspoken fears.

Positive and confident in outlook, the publication of this novel has opened a Pandora's box of insecurities; to aid his recovery you can buy this book, post positive comments wherever you can and tell all your friends.

The author has a lifetime of creative writing - mostly for job CVs, loan applications, apology letters, and internet dating sites.

Now semi-retired from 'real work', he enjoys his family and living in idyllic surroundings. He enjoys gardening, art, oysters, the world, and anything likely to enhance and extend his life.

He looks forward to creating further novels currently residing in his head, and hopes meanwhile that you will enjoy this humble offering…

FOR INDOOR AND OUTDOOR USE ONLY

John Beverley

FOR INDOOR AND OUTDOOR USE ONLY

Vanguard Press

VANGUARD PAPERBACK

© Copyright 2020
John Beverley

The right of John Beverley to be identified as author of
this work has been asserted by him in accordance with the
Copyright, Designs and Patents Act 1988.

A CIP catalogue record for this title is
available from the British Library.

ISBN 978 1 78465 755 0

*Vanguard Press is an imprint of
Pegasus Elliot Mackenzie Publishers Ltd.*
www.pegasuspublishers.com

First Published in 2020

**Vanguard Press
Sheraton House Castle Park
Cambridge England**

Printed & Bound in Great Britain

Dedication

To my family, friends and all the people I have known and will know. Although this is a work of fiction it draws on aspects of some personalities and the vast majority of locations are real. Identities have been changed to protect privacy but no humans, animals or sea creatures were harmed in the creation of this book.

She lay at rest quietly and in anticipation — waiting for him. Beautiful, elegant, and tranquil. Yet restrained in her open readiness.

For him the anticipation was almost profound. As to her anticipation, that would be impossible to describe. She was inviting and perfectly prepared.

He was not born into nobility, but she was a great queen. He had dared to dream of this moment for many years, and soon he would have intimate knowledge of her, aware that he would encounter no resistance. She would accept him willingly and openly.

It both challenged and amused him to contemplate what he was about to do. He had risen from humble beginnings in a relatively poor family and had then no aspirations or expectations. His life had opened up many opportunities and he had learned to mix in any social circle from commoner to royalty.

As the person he had been years back he could never have considered taking such an action. Even now some would view it as reckless and inappropriate.

But his childhood had contributed to a certain strength and he had become daring and decisive. As he approached his queen, he knew that it would be a meaningful and satisfying encounter.

Yet despite this confidence his excitement mounted, and his pulse quickened knowing that he would soon encounter the pleasure of entering her.

"Pretentious."

"What?"

"I said 'pretentious' because that's what it is."

"It's an accurate description and meant to be intriguing."

"We'll see. Bye for now."

Day 1

This was to be a voyage of discovery and adventure. He hoped that new things — places and experiences — would help him to rediscover some of the intense excitement and thrills that he had enjoyed in earlier life. Surely, they were still there waiting somewhere just below the surface?

His expectation was high as he entered the reception area for the journey. What had the early explorers felt as they prepared to sail to new lands, wondering if they might fall off the edge of a flat earth?

He presented his booking form, passport and vaccination certificate to the smiling Cunard receptionist, and went through security.

Of course, he understood the need to ensure the safety of the vessel and her passengers but why the need to remove laced up shoes? Could they be used to break down the door to the bridge and to threaten the captain to "Take us to Bermuda"?

"Not a problem," would be the response, "we're popping in there anyway. Be a pleasure." The shoes never go back on easily and one lace always ends up being too long, creating a tripping risk to endanger life. And having to remove belts, phones, laptops, coins etc. that had their proper place on his person was a nightmare as they never ended back in the right place. For days it always felt that he had lost things.

The process, he thought, should probably be renamed 'Insecurity'.

He walked the long gangway and together with assorted other people entered *Queen Victoria*. At first glance he formed the opinion that the average age on board was around a hundred and three and that some might even be in their final few days on this planet. As an active and fit sixty-plus year old he wondered if there would be anyone nearer his age with whom to interact.

Entering the cabin, he was pleased at the luxurious accommodation which, he concluded, might prove to be where he would choose to remain hermit-like for the entire voyage apart from leaving for meals and drinks. A useful bottle of Blanc de Blancs thoughtfully placed on ice in the cabin would no doubt lift his spirits. Funny how moods dampened by packing, travelling and fatigue could be improved by a dose of alcohol.

Having unpacked, he drank some of the chilled wine and watched the departure with fireworks from the quay at Southampton, then enjoyed a gin and tonic in one of the bars before dinner and a show. The elegant surroundings helped him feel more relaxed and he felt good about the prospect of his journey. Finally, he crashed out exhausted as the ship gently rocked in the ocean swell.

"Just confirms it. The opening is pretentious because you're describing the start of an ocean voyage with the main character a sanitised version of you."

"I was hoping it might be a great literary work, maybe ending up on bestseller lists with film rights and such, or at least required reading for schools. Be a bloody sight more interesting for kids than Shakespeare."

"Well, you can live in hope, I guess."

"Hold on, this is bizarre, who actually are you?"

"OK. Happy to oblige. How long have you got? But not at the moment. I need to be somewhere else right now. Cheerio."

He dreamt but could not recall the details other than that the dreams were happy and contented. Except one where his face had aged badly, and he was contemplating how to get it fixed.

Day 2

47.7 degrees North, 7.7 degrees West

Total nautical miles travelled by midday — 371

The alarm woke him, and he switched it off. Sleeping on for another hour he then rose and switched on the TV to check the navigational channel showing their progress. They were to the west of the Brest peninsula and still in the English Channel. There was a red line showing the route taken west of the Isle of Wight, but it showed an odd zigzag. It later transpired that the ship had stopped for a medical evacuation in the late hours, someone's dream voyage cut so short. He had no intentions of being in the same boat. Or more accurately of no longer being in it.

Crossing the Atlantic west-bound creates an extra hour some nights to adjust to the change in time zones. This had been one such night and his additional one-hour snooze was therefore excusable as it hadn't really happened. There was no justification for a guilt trip even if one could be purchased from the tour office on board. He thought it would probably be expensive anyway.

He was semi-retired after a varied career and a number of business ventures of mixed but generally good success. He lived comfortably in London and had a lifestyle that in his youth he could not even have thought might be possible.

The voyage was his retirement gift to himself and would take him to the Caribbean, and around South America for seventy-five nights, visiting briefly many places he had for some years hoped to see.

He was single and — quote — 'reasonably attractive' according to some of his friends, particularly those older ones with deteriorating eyesight. A few of these predicted that he would meet the love of his life on the trip. He thought otherwise. The love of his life was long gone, and he did not feel ready again for such a risk.

In truth the word 'single' should have been 'divorced' which he had been, twice. But he thought that 'single' was a positive word indicating some success in avoiding relationship potholes. By comparison the other word had a strongly negative feel that he did not wish to be associated with. Whenever he had used it before he had noted a fleeting look and imagined an invisible silver cross, garlic and holy water being held before him. He could not shake off the self-imposed stigma and some sense of loss from 'failing' — two times.

"That's better."

"What is?"

"How you put all that."

"Gee, oh gosh, wow… thank you so much. I'm indebted."

"Yes, you should be. Just trying to offer support but must dash… other things to do."

Day 3

42.4 degrees North, 17.3 degrees West

Total nautical miles travelled by midday — 882

When he awoke, they were west of Portugal, heading for the Azores with a heavy five to six metre ocean swell through which the ship ploughed creating clouds of spray and rolling in an interesting way.

He was thinking about how much sea there was. Being far from shore again was a strange feeling, but one that he had been well accustomed to in a former role. Even then there had been times when it focussed his thinking. It was a long way to the bottom.

"Did you really just write that last sentence?"

"Yes, what's wrong with it?"

"Hmmm."

"Hold on. This has been going on long enough. Who actually are you?"

"You could just say 'a voice in your head'."

"Or?"

"Or what?"

"Or what else could you say?"

"Listen very carefully. I'm just a voice… in your head. I don't have a head. I don't even exist in the physical sense so I'm not anything corporeal. I can't even be described as being or existing. So, by definition, I don't exist at all and, that being the case, I can't say anything more about it."

"Bollocks!"

"Did you say that. Or did I?"

"I said it."

"You sure?"

"Yes."

"Totally sure?"

"Yes! Hold on. Who's doing this?"

"This is going nowhere. Houston, we think we might have a problem. I'm off!"

The sea was getting rougher and they had been joined off the starboard side by another Cunard ship, the *Queen Elizabeth*, also heading to Bermuda, their planned first port of call. They rode the swell some distance apart as both ships pitched and rolled, spray flying wildly, with the other vessel at one time circled by a rainbow as if a portent of some mystical experience awaiting him.

He hoped that might prove to be the case.

Day 4

39.0 degrees North, 26.2 degrees West

Total nautical mile travelled by midday — 1,337

He'd had a rough night. He had slept like a baby… that is to say waking six or seven times… although not for feeding as he was enjoying more than sufficient food on board.

He recalled the theory that babies cried in the night to prevent their parents having sex. No sex = no more babies = undivided attention for the current little one = best chance of survival. He wasn't making any noise that he was aware of and he certainly wasn't crying, so he thought it unlikely that he would be affecting anyone's sexual activity in the adjoining cabins. But considering the ages of some people onboard that was probably unlikely to have caused any problems anyway — he theorised that they would also be unable to hear anything through the well soundproofed walls.

It had not been a rough night from the consumption of fizz at the commodore's black-tie cocktail reception, nor from the very palatable wine at dinner. It was a rough night because the sea had been very lumpy with high winds and swells. His sleep had been disturbed many times by the creaks, bangs and groans of the great ship as she crashed through the mid-Atlantic waves. She'd obviously hit a couple of speed bumps judging from the occasional bang and the shudder that ran through the ship. He'd learned from a fellow traveller with a career in shipping how a boat must flex at sea to avoid breaking in two. Good to know. Less good was his offer to show him the position of where some of the cracks were likely to be, although in reassuring him he said that every vessel had them.

He'd also discovered at the drinks party that there were some younger people aboard, and that those he met, including his dining companions, had interesting and colourful backgrounds too. He revised his estimate of the average age downwards to eighty-three, which might not have been too wide of the mark. There was hope and he was enjoying the company of the people he met and spoke with.

More sea, and nothing more to see apart from the sea. The sister *Queen* was no longer there. He thought that possibly she may have become bored and was taking a different route now. He would find out shortly that both ships were diverting to the Azores due to bad weather because they were unlikely to get to the intended stop at Bermuda on time or to be able to navigate the small channel to the quayside there in rough seas.

A throwaway remark by the comedian last evening pointed out how close the ship always was to land… 'downward' and no doubt that had destroyed the brief reassurance for some of the audience.

They arrived mid-afternoon in the Azores at the port of Praia da Vitoria on the island of Terceira and he went ashore for a few hours to walk around the delightful town before returning to the boat for dinner and an early night to catch up on sleep. He was enjoying himself.

"Bit more relaxed, are you?"

"I like rough seas."

"Wasn't talking about that. You're not as stressed as just before the trip."

"Isn't that how it's meant to be?"

"Guess so. Life on the ocean wave… more fine living… I'm having a great time!"

"I thought we were going to explore further what's going on here."

"Fine, but not now. Got to be somewhere else. See you."

Day 5

38.4 degrees North, 27.3 degrees West

Total nautical miles travelled by midday — not known — still in port — unable to depart due to high winds.

He was woken by an announcement from the commodore that they would be sailing early due to continued bad weather. Shore leave was cancelled even for passengers. Rain and high winds were sweeping across the quay and he watched as a large shipping container on the dock was blown several feet sideways by the wind. The first attempt to sail failed because the wind was blowing the ship against the quay and the ship came alongside again. Several sun loungers from the top rear deck were blown overboard.

This was going to be an interesting leg of the journey.

"So now you want to be a travel writer?"

"Go away, I'm too busy for this."

"Bit of a role reversal you being the busy one but there you go. I'm gone. Bye!"

His thoughts formed. He had, he reflected, been born quite young and he had also managed to stay young for quite a few of his early years, innocent and learning to be both self-contained and sociable. An only child but by no means a lonely child although at one stage he would have liked a brother or sister as many of his friends had. Someone to share a view of the world with... and hit sometimes.

He knew that he was an accident. Not a failure of birth control, but like every person living on this planet a chance collection of genetics that could have resulted in him being someone entirely different. He felt special but came to learn in later life that he could be both this and completely ordinary. Special and ordinary was OK. He had read when he was older about DNA research on the roots of humankind, and who his ancient ancestors might be. In particular he was fascinated that Neanderthal man (and woman no doubt) had bigger brains. The big question was, what for? And what could they do that we cannot? DNA research showed from our genes that modern man had mated with Neanderthals, but there was no way of knowing if they had the ability to speak. Perhaps, he thought, they simply couldn't say 'no' to a chat-up line from Homo Sapiens.

In addition, there were theories that modern man may have actually eaten Neanderthals to the point of their extinction. Like some spiders after mating? 'I'd like to nibble your ear darling' suddenly becomes sinister and why in heaven's name would you want to eat your lovers? Except, he considered, it might save on meal costs of post-coital dinner. And avoid an evening of zero conversation — although this was something that many modern human couples still seemed quite capable of doing.

His childhood had been uneventful. At primary school, age five, he had written and directed a small comedy playlet and performed this with friends at the morning assembly. 'A Mouse in the House' featured an extremely deaf very old man. 'Directed' is a specific word and the friends, no doubt spurred by stage adrenaline and their tender ages, had hijacked the performance by shamelessly ad-libbing and modifying the script beyond recognition so that the headmistress had to abort the whole thing as it started to spiral out of control. The loss to British theatre can only be imagined.

In reality, he had no vision of the theatre or of anything else as a future. No one helped him to have any vision, not parents, relatives, or teachers. How could they, when they had just emerged from World War II and life seemed pretty much to be about surviving and rebuilding? So he just lived, happily and contentedly in Salford making tar babies with his friends on hot days from melting tarmac, dust from the roadside, matchstick arms and legs, and stone chipping eyes. Did the artist Lowry maybe see them and take inspiration? And, when it snowed, they made snowmen.

"Definitely Freudian this bit."

"What are you on about?"

"Creating people. Babies and snowmen. Wanting to procreate. Needing to pass on your gene pool."

"Oh, please… just go away for now. You remind me of the man whose psychiatrist showed him a series of Rorschach inkblots and was answered with something sexual for each image. When he challenged the man about his interpretation the man accused him of continually showing him dirty pictures."

"I'm off, I think I need to go and look at some of those right now."

His education was mixed and impacted by having to change schools several times as the family moved with his father's job. From the north to the south of the country not only having to adapt to a new curriculum but also having to learn to speak again in the local dialect in order to be understood. But better still was being dropped into a Latin class at the back of the classroom with a textbook in Year 2 and being told to catch up unaided on the year he had missed. As a result, he spoke Latin as well as any Roman legionnaire. Being dead they could no longer speak it either.

The little Latin he did absorb was occasionally useful, for example, understanding the alternative comedic narrative of vidi, vici, veni. But he was still unsure of the value of knowing the language and the legacy of the invasion, recalling the Essex graffiti he'd seen years back which succinctly said 'The Romans came to Colchester in AD 43 and fuck all has happened since.'

Eventually the ship escaped as the wind abated marginally and they sailed mid-afternoon, heading south-west into more rough waters to leave the Azores heading for Florida. Bermuda had disappeared — they would not be seeing it.

Drinks, dinner, conversation, a show in the theatre, and then sleep. This was becoming a pattern. But a very pleasant one.

Day 6

36.2 degrees North, 35.0 degrees West

Total nautical miles travelled by midday — 1,807

Another sleep-interrupted night with the noises of the heavy seas from nine-metre waves, but he woke as planned. Planned not only as to the time of waking but because part of his regular planning every night was to wake the next morning. It was his simple method of living to a ripe old age. You can't be dead when you're alive. He had been described as distinguished and had no desire to be called extinguished.

He had no intention of dying in his sleep, nor for that matter did he wish to die in anyone else's sleep. For him, the plan was to live to 320 and then review the situation. He knew from his life that aiming high tended to produce better outcomes. As to the method of passing, his preferred options remained as they had been for many years:

Falling off a tall woman.

Driving a Harley Davidson into a lamp post in the South of France.

It followed that if he avoided motorbikes and Nice, as well as unaided climbing attempts involving Nordic ladies, that he could avoid death. QED. (Quod erat demonstrandum — thus it is proven). Some other bits of Latin had obviously stuck.

His time onboard was filled by activities, talks, and films plus the books he had brought with him. The staff were attentive and friendly — apparently numbering around one for every two of the 1,700 guests. As he had been opening his cabin on the first night, a chambermaid had welcomed him by name. He had acknowledged to her the skill it took to do that, and some waiters had also done the same. A simple but effective way of making guests feel important. He had dated some people who had been unable to do either of those things — remembering his name, or making him feel good. He had not dated them more than once.

The Atlantic Ocean was as impressive as he recalled, containing a very considerable amount of water and covering about one fifth of the planet. Its depth is significant, and he liked to be crossing it on the surface, which he hoped would continue. It obviously also contained a great number of fish and other sea creatures which could roam freely about the oceans all around the planet with no borders, passport controls or security checks to be concerned about.

Given those advantages he wondered what the motivation had been, millions of years back, for things to crawl out onto the land where they would ultimately need to invent transport to get around. And then travel agents and websites to show them where to go.

Not much of an argument for evolution he thought. Might we sometime move back into the sea if the land masses become too crowded to sustain us? He still had a snorkel and fins from a holiday. They might prove to be useful one day.

With time on his hands he watched the ocean — the big waves, the white spray from the bows, the immensity of the horizon, distant rain squalls, and so many rainbows, surely more good portents... and ghosts appeared. Not creepy dead things but rather phantoms of thoughts and memories from the past creeping and in some cases elbowing their way into his thoughts. An onboard talk on Voodoo in Haiti may have triggered this with the belief that spirits of several types guided our lives either positively or mischievously.

He recalled something from an English literature lesson about a tall ship and celestial navigation methods. A classmate thought the author had been Jayne Mansfield.

"Very poetic."

"Should be, I remembered it from school — Masefield I think, rather than the voluptuous glamour model of my schoolfriend's fantasies."

"Well you're on deck 8 with two more decks above you so that certainly justifies a definition of tall."

"But I assume they use more than the stars for navigation."

"Certainly hope so."

He started to dress in his formal wear for another cocktail reception with the commodore, along with several hundred others. Not like his time at sea. This guy must spend a serious chunk of his job socialising and drinking. He wondered about the career path to such things. Nobody at school had told him about such possibilities but then no teacher or careers master at that time would have been on any ship other than the navy or merchant navy, and at war rather than swanning around indulging themselves. And doubtless working hard too.

He thought about his father being captured in North Africa and taken on an Italian prisoner of war ship across the Mediterranean only to be bombed by the RAF and to survive that then to see the soldier in front of him on the beach be killed by a cannon shell through the neck. A lump rose in his throat at the recollection because his father had said so little about the war until he was dying of liver cancer.

"Not nice at all."

"It wasn't. But all that just came out from nowhere. Another 'ghost'."

"So, perhaps some guilt from never speaking with your father about it?"

"Well, yes… maybe."

"It fucking should be… excuse me, please, got to go."

The other part of that story was that his father had stolen the brass key to the Italian captain's cabin as he escaped the ship. To his shame he had never asked his father why… and never asked if he had locked the captain in… he didn't think his father would have done such a thing, but personally as a son with a different life he, at the same age in his early twenties, might well have.

The key still hung proudly on the wall of his study.

Day 7

34.0 degrees North, 45.0 degrees West

Total nautical miles covered by midday — 2,318

The sea was becoming calmer and he had slept well. They had passed the longest mountain range in the world, unnoticed as it was beneath the sea.

He allowed the ghosts to return and childhood memories surfaced slowly. For a period covering so many years they were relatively few. He remembered some of his small friends in the street but oddly he could not recall friends from junior school, nor the names of his teachers. He remembered pets and snowy days tobogganing, plus thick 'pea soup' fogs so bad that he covered his mouth and nose with a handkerchief and scarf. When the handkerchief was removed it was stained yellow from tar and grime. On one occasion, he had become totally disorientated crossing a road because he could not see more than a few inches in the disgusting greenish yellow swirling mist. When he encountered the pavement on the other side it wasn't where it should have been. He remembered the event vividly but not how he eventually got home.

And he remembered a vivid yellow coloured medicine by taste and smell, and the dentist where gas-anaesthetic induced nightmares of brutal warfare.

After lunch he lost a few dollars at roulette but became bored and went to the bar. Scanning the drinks list he saw a cocktail for his star sign of Cancer. The description read 'Refined, elegant and sensitive yet sensational, ambitious and stirring.' How could he resist such an accurate description of his own personality? He knew full well that it was a technique of psychology much used in horoscopes whereby people relate to positive things they believe are written about them. Despite this he still thought it was spot on — incredibly perceptive and true, and very much him. Self-delusion comes easily as one ages.

He ordered the cocktail and drank the cold rum and fruit mixture from a ceramic pot in the shape of an elephant, trying not to let fellow passengers see the absurd drinking vessel. He noted that the personality description had not said 'easily embarrassed in some situations'.

Another full day of talks, classes and options including one entitled 'Is your hair saying the right thing about you?' Being almost totally bald he considered how his attendance might affect the discussion if he showed up, but he decided in the end not to go but instead to make an appointment next day for a haircut.

He was curious to see what the effect might be.

Day 8

32.3 degrees North, 54.6 degrees West

Total nautical miles covered by midday — 2,816

Calmer seas, scattered cloud and the air getting warmer with two days to go until Florida and the crew now dressed in tropical white uniforms.

They were entering the Sargasso Sea, which he recalled from childhood as being a place where ships became becalmed. A place also famous for its seaweed which could be seen floating in increasing amounts, apparently where four currents met, creating a fairly motionless middle bit of ocean 3,200 kilometres long by 1,100 kilometres wide. A place for eels, he thought. What he hadn't known about was the appearance of the sea here as it was his first trip to this area. The water was incredibly clear and a deep translucent blue.

An uneventful day ended with a show featuring an antipodean singer, the highlight of which was an operatic aria. As he listened, he thought it could have been renamed 'Possum Dorma', and had it been translated as 'None Shall Sheep' he would have treasured that.

"That was definitely pushing it. I'll leave you with that observation. Goodnight!"

"Sleep well!"

"Always do, thank you."

Day 9

30.9 degrees North, 64.3 degrees West

Total nautical miles covered by midday — 3,294

Under cover of darkness in the early hours, they had slipped unnoticed into the Bermuda Triangle. Lit only by faint starlight they had ignored the warning signs — 'Danger. Restricted Area. No Entry. Turn Back. Survivors May Be Prosecuted etc. etc.' The border guards had obviously been dozing.

He had been asleep so had not seen any of this, nor the dotted fluorescent lines atop the ocean marking the boundary to the no-go area as shown in the maps in literature about this place.

He had read the book in his very early teens when conspiracy theories abounded. The supposed triangle pattern matched the shape of the sides of the pyramids, also supposed to confer magical properties although to his knowledge very few ships had been lost in the Egyptian desert. And the profile of Toblerone bars, where nothing to his knowledge had been lost except perhaps good intentions of dieting after Christmas.

In reality he knew the statistics around which the book was based were questionable but what did that matter when the book had sold very successfully, and he had enjoyed it?

It was around this time in his early teens that his appetite and thirst for knowledge was at its peak. He devoured books.

"Come on, 'devour'… you didn't actually eat the books. Why not say you drank books to quench your thirst for information?"

"Well it's an interesting observation about the English language."

"Happy to assist. Bye, must get on, other things to do."

He had by now made the move to the south coast with his parents and started in a new secondary school. He mixed well despite the language barrier of northern and southern English dialects. Perhaps his new friends found him interesting because initially it was necessary to repeat so much, both ways.

Over several months they formed a regular gang although it never had a name or any initiation ceremonies. It just formed itself between a group of boys who related to each other. They acquired nicknames that again somehow evolved or simply appeared one day. He was known as 'Brilliance' because of his way of stating the blindingly obvious with some sort of satirical or ironic slant. His friends, for now forgotten reasons, had been 'Sunshine', 'Dill' and 'Moonshine'. He had little doubt that they would have been very successful in whatever careers they had chosen, in one case due to the frightening intellect and an ability to excel at every subject without doing any work.

He remembered little of school except those teachers who left an impression from the couple of subjects he enjoyed. When it came to career choices, he envied those who knew what they wanted to be when they grew up. He had been asked that question so many times as a very young child and had given the then standard answer from the *Beano* or some similar comic of 'a train driver'. It was the sort of answer expected of young boys at the time.

He couldn't now use it as a stock response because he definitely no longer wanted to do that. It might have kept him on the right track, but it would take him to limited places only. The job of an airline pilot appealed marginally but he really had no idea and anything interesting or exotic seemed beyond his reach.

He remembered one boy, adept at biology and possibly with medical connections in the family, who rather smugly had told the careers master in front of the whole class that he wished to become a gynaecologist. Pausing only briefly the master had said, 'Wouldn't bother, Peters, you'd never find the right openings.' A few in the class recognised the humour and stifled their laughter. For others, including Peters, the brilliance of the response was lost.

He was unable to get to grips with history as a subject. He could not link dates to events, and he had little interest in what had already long passed. Maths, however, was the opposite and he intuitively knew when calculations were correct even to a number of decimal places — the answer felt right. It was a mystical and fascinating subject for him.

For this reason, his first job had nothing at all to do with mathematics. Probably how it goes for most people.

Day 10

28.9 degrees North, 73.7 degrees West

Total nautical miles travelled by midday — 3,768

More sea. It was probably to be expected on an ocean voyage. The final transatlantic day and by Florida they would have covered around 4,200 nautical miles and gone almost one fifth of the way around the world.

The calculation was based upon the circumference of the earth at the equator which was actually not the route that they had taken. They were on a different track involving part of the 'great circle', an apparent straight line which curves across the surface of the spherical globe that is the earth. But he remembered that it is not actually a sphere at all but rather an oblate spheroid flattened slightly at the poles and stretched at the equator. That meant that a proper calculation would take him some time and might involve web searches, eating into the limited internet browsing time for which he was paying. To be precise he only paid for the excess over the allowance provided, but the money for this excess was earmarked for more important things like laundry, drinks and excursions.

"You're doing it again. Maths is eating your brain. Stop. You really do need to get a life sometimes. Got to run. Bye!"

He calculated that if he had driven this route (allowing for the small technical detail that there was no road) it would have taken almost the same time assuming covering an average of 500 land miles per day, and allowing for stopping for food, drink, bathrooms, changes of clothes, and sleep.

Turning to the costs — allowing for fuel, food and drink, wear and tear on the vehicle, and places to sleep, and offsetting an allowance for the saving of electricity, gas and other domestic items not used at home — it probably came out almost at break-even with the voyage cost. He could create a complex spreadsheet and formulae to justify this but in his mathematical mind he knew that the answer would be very similar.

"I thought I'd said to stop all this mathematical stuff. Must dash, cheerio."

Several people on the ship considered it cheaper on board than a residential care home and seemed to spend much of their life cruising the globe.

Knowing now the cost-effectiveness of cruising, he headed straight to the voyage sales office to discuss future options. The lady was very helpful. She was nowhere near eighty-three. And she had very nice legs.

And he knew that he really did need to get a life.

Day 11

28.2 degrees North, 78.6 degrees West

Total nautical miles travelled by midday — 4,006

"You can't say that — it's sexist."

"Can't say what?"

"About the lady's legs."

"That was yesterday."

"I know, but I've been busy."

"Well I think I can justify saying it as it's factual and, in any case, a male friend of mine told me recently that I have good legs, so it's just an observation unrelated to gender."

"I'll skip my observation on your friend but maybe you should be a little concerned... see you!"

They had docked before dawn at Port Canaveral, Florida. It was cold. Florida shouldn't be like that.

To disembark for a tour everyone had been advised that it might take some time because US immigration would want to interview all the passengers. But disappointingly, they didn't ask him anything about his interests, which book he'd read last, his favourite author, what prejudices he had, his last job, or any clever psychological stuff like 'is this a good question?' He must have passed anyway because they let him in without any hassle or delay. Perhaps the immigration guy had noticed his legs?

He took a guided tour of the Kennedy Space Centre, a good name he thought because there certainly was a lot of room judging by the amount of unspoiled wilderness in which it was located. In some ways it reflected former glories of the moon shot etc. But alongside that he saw a commercial rocket on the launchpad, which would take off within days and then return to land rather than having to be recovered or wasted. A stated objective of NASA and others was to reach Mars within a few years. It seemed that man was again ready to push the boundaries of exploration as far as advancing technology would permit. Currently it was as though our exploration of the universe had only gone as far as the first millimetre of the front doorstep of the house in which we live, not even out into the garden. So much for the idea of returning to the oceans, there were obviously bigger fish to fry.

He ate in one of the restaurants and decided that he needed to find a manager to ask how, with NASA's reputation for excellence in pushing the boundaries of science, they could manage to produce a cheese pizza that was virtually inedible. It wasn't exactly rocket science. He threw a piece to the birds outside and they ignored it. The bus was, however, waiting and he had no time for something that unimportant in the midst of so much positivity and inspiration.

After the ship had sailed, he watched the receding lights from the shore and slept well.

Day 12

26.5 degrees North, 80.7 degrees West

Total nautical miles travelled by midday — 4,164

He awoke to find the ship docked at Port Everglades (Fort Lauderdale), Florida. It was again very cold. Thoughts of climate change emerged.

Several hundred passengers would disembark here making way for an intake, he feared, of blue rinse Floridian widows in assorted larger sizes. Time would tell if he was right, but he did have some prior insight of this species and their behaviour on ships.

The ship filled up on fuel and provisions during the day while he took a bus ride to see the city. It was elegant and expensive, particularly along the seashore where many luxury hotels had been built. On the inland waterways there were boats of varying sizes from modest to colossal. The combined cost of these would be in the billions of dollars and, in some cases, they were moored alongside equally large and expensive waterside properties. He knew he would witness more like this on the next part of the voyage. Well, somebody had to do it and relatively speaking he as an observer was a pauper.

Some guests told him they had been on a tour of Miami and seen the homes of stars and the wealthy, including the inventor of Viagra. That property would no doubt continue to stand firmly in even the most severe hurricanes.

In the afternoon they departed for Grand Turk in the Turks and Caicos Islands via the Bahamas, and some of his old hunting grounds.

"Strange expression. 'Hunting grounds."

"I thought you'd gone away?"

"No, I just went ashore. Things I wanted to see."

As they sailed in the darkness, white birds alighted on the waves from the bow, presumably eating small fish or creatures churned up by the wake. As the ship progressed, the birds at the rear of the ship flew to the front in an ongoing repetitive cycle.

Some symbolism here? he wondered.

Day 13

24.7 degrees North, 75.4 degrees West

Total nautical miles travelled by midday — 4,444

He awoke to see land on the horizon, one of the islands of the Bahamas. It was warmer — slightly. On the ship were a series of displays of Cunard history including one showing part of the story of the building of a liner he remembered from his early teens — the *QE2*, which he had seen on her sea trials off the south coast of England. There had been many thefts by shipyard workers apparently pushing the building cost up dramatically. One arrested worker had been found to have removed many things which were discovered on a search of his home by the police, including (but not limited to):

3 lounge stools

30 yards of carpet

55 metres of fibreglass

107 metres of electric cable

2 chests of drawers

4 settee backs

3 bookcases

1 toilet seat

Two questions arose in his mind:

How did he smuggle them from the shipyard — presumably not in his lunchbox?

What did his house look like as it was obvious that his skills at interior design were non-existent?

And then the ghosts returned with recollections about stealing apples, and pressure from his peer group to steal pencils from Woolworths. The combined results of years of teenagers stealing from their stores may well have contributed to the business failing. But the biggest memory was a story from his early teen years.

One balmy summer evening in Sussex, he and his neighbourhood friends were walking and chatting as they often did, heading the couple of miles to the sea. On the way, and abandoned in the rough grass at the roadside, was a battered and rusting old bike. They picked it up and discovered that it was still in rideable condition so that it accompanied them to the beach as they took turns riding it. Heading out to sea from the pebbly beach was an outfall pipe encased in timber and from which they used to dive and swim, and catch once a large conger eel. The tide was coming in and would soon submerge the pipe. It was only logical to them to ride the bike along the pipe in turns and into the water, and this they did many times until the depth of the water made it impossible to retrieve the bike.

It was innocent fun, playing stunt riders like something from an adventure film and they walked home as dusk fell, tired and happy.

Many years later he was recounting the tale when he was hit as if by lightning with a blinding flash of the totally bloody obvious. They had deprived someone of their bicycle. Possibly someone older (a high probability as this was Sussex) and poor (as they must have been with a bike like that), whose bike was their only means of transport (local buses didn't go that way and being poor they couldn't have afforded the bus fare let alone a car), plus this bike would certainly have been passed down through countless generations and would undoubtedly have enormous sentimental value to the owner. (Or more correctly, former owner). As if this were not enough, they would not, by definition, have had the money to buy a replacement bike.

He was racked with remorse. There was nothing he could now do. But also, by the way that four boys had not seen it in that light at the time believing it to be a totally innocent action. He imagined how their explanation to a magistrate would have sounded, and what the consequences might have been if they had been branded as child offenders. Without question their futures could well have been changed.

Mid-afternoon they passed the last of the islands in the Bahamas. He thought that they were probably now out of the Bermuda Triangle without consequence. The slightly hungover feeling and dull headache this morning had possibly been as a result of an alien abduction in the night, but he had no memories and so the aliens had obviously done this well. He would check over dinner with the new American guests. He'd read that a very high percentage of Americans claimed to have experienced abductions, often involving sexual experimentation.

It would be interesting to compare notes with some of the newly arrived passengers.

Day 14

21.2 degrees North, 71.8 degrees West

Total nautical miles travelled by midday — 4,614

"Sex."

"I see you're back. What do you want?"

"More sex. The story needs more of it if it's going to sell."

"Thank you. I'm glad you raised that as he's about to enter that time of his life and I'm concerned. I may need help."

"OK. I'm listening."

"But who/what are you exactly?"

"Already told you — a voice in your head, and if you ask 'what voice' the answer is 'this one'. But I could also be other things... like your conscience, for example, and/or your muse."

"Why are you only now telling me that?"

"You weren't ready to hear it. And I've been busy doing other stuff."

"Just for clarity, you're saying that my mind is saying that my mind wasn't prepared for what my mind thought?"

"Close as you're going to get. What help do you need?"

"I'm worried about writing in detail about sex in case my children read this."

"No problem."

"How can it not be a problem? I'm very anxious."

"Simple. You aren't writing it. I am. Your muse, your subconscious, your alter ego, your doppelgänger. Blame me/us/them. I promise you it won't be a problem."

"Unless we get a conflict between the family over any copyright and profits."

Sex. It was the swinging sixties. The music was sexual and exciting, rock groups abounded, ties were floral, girls were pretty, mini-skirts were in fashion, alcohol flowed freely at parties, life was cool. Provided he pooled money with his mates to buy cheap beer and cider and could gatecrash a party when they found out where one was, then the weekends, for sure, were fun even if weekdays were mostly education and boredom.

There were only a few informal rules about partying:

1. It was absolutely essential not to know the person whose house the party was in. Otherwise it could prove to be embarrassing.

2. The location of the party must have come via someone knowing someone who'd heard from a friend of a friend, or someone in the pub etc. That would ensure maximum attendance and total anonymity.

3. The person holding the party (henceforth to be known as the crashee) would admit anyone who turned up (henceforth to be known as the crasher/s).

4. The parents of the crashee must be away for the weekend, or preferably longer. World cruises ranked highly.

5. Lots of drink must be taken by all crashers to pool with all other alcohol at the party whether the crashee's, his parent's, or the crashers. The ratio varied but parental booze was often plentiful and better quality if it could be located. That required effort and imagination. Sometimes prized scotch was hidden in rabbit hutches and the like, but mostly in sheds where fathers hung out.

6. Drinking from other people's glasses, cups or bottles was an absolute requirement.

7. Dancing without abandon to the latest LPs was enforced, until it was no longer possible to stand let alone move around vertically.

8. Sleeping in the parents' bed was completely taboo and so must be undertaken by virtually everyone, whether for sex, to pass out, or for any other purpose.

9. Condoms must be worn at all times.

10. Sex was freely available.

11. Drugs flowed freely and were to be shared.

The problem with these rules was limited only to the last three.

Rule 11 — There were usually no drugs, maybe some weed if lucky but in such small quantities it would only affect the actual smoker with perhaps secondary effects on the crashee's pet budgerigar when smoked near the cage.

Rules 10 and 11 — sex for him and many of his friends was quite limited in reality, making the condom rule an irrelevance.

And the one final and absolute rule —

12. Crashers must leave the party next day after sleeping off hangovers etc. without assisting the crashee to rebuild or refurnish the property. His or her excuse to the returning parents would be that the intimate party of close school friends, 'no more than five, I promise' had been gate-crashed by thugs who had forced their way in, drugged the family dog, and shouted insults at the budgie creating all the untold damage while holding the crashee at gunpoint or knifepoint as well as threatening physical violence — and 'they were much bigger and older'... and 'no, he definitely couldn't identify them which is why he hadn't called the police'...

He was at Grand Turk for only a few hours and the rain was lashing and torrential in the morning although he did snorkel in rough seas and meet a sting rat. The predictive text on his laptop spelt it that way as he wrote an email to a friend before the actual sting rat encounter. A sting ray was one thing, and very beautiful, but the concept of a sting rat was far more enticing and threatening.

He returned to the ship to change from soaking clothes — it had been wetter on the snorkelling boat than in the sea he thought — and then he caught a taxi to town for a quick view of the island.

The taxi driver was named Moses. Funny how coincidences happen. He told driver Moses that he had seen the real Moses in Egypt a few months prior on a Nike cruise. Repeat Nike. The predictive text had done that too renaming a river with thousands of years of history with the brand name of a trainer created only a very few years ago! The real Moses he had seen was walking by a jetty beside the Nike in flowing robes with a large white beard and long unkempt white hair. He had his possessions wrapped in a blanket around his shoulders on top of which perched a very big cat looking nonchalantly around. He wasn't sure if this should have been a mystical experience or if it had actually been the real Moses, but Moses 2 the taxi driver certainly enjoyed the story.

The afternoon was sunnier, and he found Grand Turk to be very attractive with pastel coloured buildings and warm, friendly people. What he hadn't expected was the extent of damage caused by two recent hurricanes, far more than the media had stated when they reported the total devastation in other islands. A considerable amount of damage was obviously not as newsworthy as total destruction. He wondered how long it would take for repairs to be completed and whether they could do this before the next hurricane season, only a few months away.

The boat sailed late afternoon into high winds and more heavy seas.

Day 15

19.3 degrees North, 65.2 degrees West

Total nautical miles travelled by midday — 4,968

"Remember the sex."

"OK, I'll try to pay it more attention."

"You need to if this book is going to sell. See you!"

It was a sea day as they sailed through the Caribbean. He owed an apology to the Americans. He had not seen any blue rinses and only a few signs of obesity.

Continuing his teen memories, a number of random thoughts surfaced. Spontaneous erections on the upper deck of the bus to school, which he had tried to conceal by clutching his school bag to his groin as he descended the steps to get off at the school stop, and the recognition of precisely how un-swinging the 1960s had been for him and his friends. They had tried to pretend otherwise particularly when reporting to each other the scoring from the previous night's encounters with girls.

There was a points system from 1 — kissing, to 10 — full sex with specific numbers between for various 'ascending' activities. Most boys reported at least 1 or 2 higher than reality which undoubtedly increased both peer pressure to perform better and feelings of inadequacy. The girls he knew used the same system but probably reported at least 1 point lower than reality. This latter information came via the sisters of boys he knew. It had the side benefit of creating short lists of girls worthy of trying to get to know. Unfortunately, there was always a stigma attached to dating a friend's sister perhaps because the friend did not or could not see his sister as sexual or attractive.

Teenage pregnancies were real no-go areas, heavily publicised by teachers, parents, and the press. The fact that such pregnancies were limited may have had something to do with the difficulty of 'going on the pill' — oral contraception required a visit to a doctor and sometimes the need for parental consent. It seemed some doctors were not disposed to prescribing such things, and therefore the fear of pregnancy itself proved to be a very effective method of contraception. In some cases, sexual ignorance actually worked too — thinking you could become pregnant by passionate kissing, for example, limited the exploratory behaviour of some girls.

Condoms could only be purchased over the counter from chemists. For fourteen-year-olds, this was a rite of passage. Every boy had to have some in case he got lucky, kept in a wallet to display if proof were needed, and possessing some came, it was believed, with a cast-iron guarantee of sex. It was, of course, believed wrongly and any chat-up line including reference to the possession of a pack of condoms invariably failed for some reason. "I've got a condom... how about it?" never seemed to work. It was the sister of a school friend who gently and sympathetically made him aware of the inadequacy of this chat-up line with her quiet response of "Fuck off".

He had himself stood embarrassed in the local chemist looking at toothbrushes and waiting for the male chemist to be free, only for the older, sour-faced lady chemist to ask forcibly what he wanted. It was, at that stage of his life, his most embarrassing moment. The next one was a few minutes later when his friends waiting outside had asked how it had gone and forced him to hand over the small paper bag containing the purchase. Opening this revealed a pack of sticking plasters. "Oh well," one had commented, "I suppose you could just tape her over."

Later they learned that many gent's hairdressers carried a stock of condoms and would discreetly ask at the till if the gentleman required 'something for the weekend'. It was not generally offered to under-age youths and even if it had been the probable response of 'got any tickets for the match?' would have been a major embarrassment in a shop crowded by older males.

As a result of all this, good girls simply did not indulge. The focus, therefore, had to be on finding the other type, and many boys devoted much time to that rather than studying.

Passing at some distance the mostly unseen islands of Dominican Republic, Puerto Rico, US and British Virgin Islands, Anguilla, Antigua and Barbuda, Guadeloupe, and Dominica, he was taken back in time to his days working on cruise liners in this part of the world.

His first job as trainee manager of a supermarket and his subsequent promotions had not been fulfilling. As a small child, he had been taught by his grandmother to play the piano as well as learning many songs from the First World War onwards, plus a couple of wind instruments which he also played — badly. But he could sing. He performed with a number of amateur operatic societies and married from that circle. The marriage bore two children, one of whom died very young, and the marriage broke not least because he had met one of those other type of girls at work and become a fan of the uninhibited sex they stole together. He recognised now that he was partly driven by the thrill of the chase and the intrigue.

Following the break-up of the marriage he had changed direction and gained work with *ACE Lines* — American Cruise Excursions to give it the full name — a group registered in one of the Caribbean islands and operating a few small vessels for mostly American travellers. He gained employment with the help of a personal contact from his light operatic group who had become a singer on one of their vessels. A new life with new experiences awaited. He wanted to grab life by the throat and shake it, and he worked very hard at doing exactly that. He maintained contact as best he could with his daughter whom he missed enormously, sending postcards of exotic places and writing to her as well as making regular phone calls when the sometimes primitive, international phone systems on the islands permitted this. She lived with her mother and was happy to see him when he had shore leave in the UK.

He could already do some basic dance steps and needed to get his dancing up to speed for the new job, so he enrolled for a crash course with the *Sylvia Rogers Dance Academy* in Birkenhead and within two intensive weeks he had the requisite skills. This proved to be one of his best investments in terms of the returns from the initial outlay of a few hundred pounds and some delightful company with some of his dance partners.

As night fell on his current life, he stood on deck to watch the sunset, the stars and the sliver of crescent moon, as well as the lights of distant islands. It would have been very romantic in the right circumstances.

But he doubted he would ever encounter those right circumstances again.

Day 16

14.3 degrees North, 61.3 degrees West

Total nautical miles travelled by midday — 5,357

He awoke as the ship approached Martinique in a flat calm, and docked. Going ashore, he joined a random group to hire a taxi to see some of the island. His first impression was of the size of the port city of Fort-de-France but then as they headed into the hills on twisting roads, he saw the colourful hillside houses and towns, and the greenery and birds of the rainforest. It was a large island and in one short day they could not hope to do it justice. Nevertheless, he met interesting and friendly local people and saw sugar cane plantations and animals.

He heard about the volcanic eruption in 1902 which had destroyed the town of St. Pierre killing an estimated 30,000 people. And how in the early 1600s the Carib Indian inhabitants of the islands had been exterminated within twenty years. After that the French, unsurprisingly, encountered no further resistance from the Indians. Instead it was time for the British and Dutch who took playful turns to try to steal it, until France finally took it back again and refused to play any more.

As with so many of the islands here the story was a simple one of out-and-out theft, combined with the taking of completely innocent people as slaves, or just killing them. The death tolls in total would make Stalin look restrained.

And it made stealing a bicycle seem very trivial.

"Social conscience at work here? But it's not me, so it must be something else."

"You're implying it's another bit of my mind?"

"Must be — it definitely ain't me."

"That's more than a little worrying."

"To whom? Which bit of you is concerned? I'll leave you to work on that. See you later."

Day 17

13.6 degrees North, 59.3 degrees West

Total nautical miles travelled by midday — 5,481

They were alongside in Barbados as he awoke at six thirty — just down the road really, at only 123.7 nautical miles from Martinique.

He took a tour of some of the historic parts of the island, stolen way back by the British from the local Indians but somehow kept by the British until independence in 1966. He didn't think that made any difference as theft was theft. How would it be if he and a bunch of buddies bowled up and took Necker Island for themselves? He didn't think the owner would be too happy and he thought Sir Richard might even make him give up all his Virgin air miles as punishment.

It was a pretty island with pastel coloured houses away from Bridgetown but the traffic jams were a surprise as was the information that *McDonald's* has failed here, although *Burger King* had survived. He could find no message in that.

Three cruise liners were in port with a few thousand passengers let loose on the island, looking for experiences and things to buy. For the islanders it was like harvesting the island's staple crop of sugar cane — it was a seasonable thing, and for the Caribbean islands the months of November to March were the harvest months for cruise passenger income. For the remainder of the year only around one cruise boat per week visited the islands and life was decidedly harder.

The excesses of a life spent cruising were, he reflected, in marked contrast.

Day 18

9.9 degrees North, 54.9 degrees West

Total nautical miles travelled by midday — 5,823

He was at sea again, a beautiful sunlit morning with white flecks on the waves as they sailed towards Brazil paralleling the coasts of Guyana, Suriname and French Guiana, and to the east of Trinidad.

He watched enchanted at the flashes of the silver bodies of flying fish leaping from the water to skim just above the waves until they splashed back into the ocean. He knew that they did that to escape predators, and a large liner must appear very dangerous to such small things.

He was well aware of the theory of evolution, of natural selection, and survival of the best adapted or adaptive but he had some problems when it came to some species, and flying fish sat firmly in that camp. His logic was summarised as follows:

Day 1 of the evolutionary process for flying fish. Ordinary fish number 1 is being pursued by big toothy monster predator fish. In panic, ordinary fish, realising that there is absolutely nowhere to escape and in an instant of absolute desperation, leaps for the sky. Of course he doesn't know it is sky, just a sort of glass ceiling on his expectations. He flicks his tail, and giving everything he has, clears the water, and disappears momentarily from big toothy monster predator fish. Neither have experienced this before — it has never occurred in the entire universe and hence it can be classed as a successful outcome. Ten out of ten for ingenuity and eleven out of ten for survival technique.

Big toothy monster predator fish mentally aborts the pursuit — 'WTF' — and ordinary fish number 1 survives to tell the tale. Which he does that evening at the local meeting point of his ordinary fish friends in the fish equivalent of the local bar on the reef. The result is that the brighter ordinary fish adopt this procedure, and the lady ordinary fish are drawn to the cleverer gentlemen ordinary fish who can do this neat trick.

They also figure these clever fish will be around longer as partners. There is no need for any mention of condoms as a chat-up line.

Result — no sex for unadaptive ordinary fish = no babies = extinction, while on the other side of the equation adaptive ordinary fish gets lots of sex and breeds like crazy = survival of the best adapted. And then the ones who happen to have bigger fins get to fly further meaning that they don't land slap bang in front of big toothy monster predator fish which has also wised up from experience and learned just to continue swimming until disappearing lunch reappears with a plop, conveniently placed to simply open the mouth and swallow. Equals less energy expenditure for predator fish.

Then bigger and bigger fins are favoured, permitting longer and longer flight as part of an ongoing process until they decide instead that it would be safer to get the hell out of the sea which is full of big toothy monster predator fishes, and head for the land which is flowing with milk and honey.

Big fins turn into limbs and they simply walk ashore like tourists.

Pretty much Darwin's theory, he thought, but he had spotted several flaws, not least that to his knowledge there were still plenty more fish in the sea that had survived without ever sprouting wings or moving ashore. And, why hadn't big toothy monster fishes just learned to flick their tails and take to the air too, creating maybe the first ever in-flight meal?

"Neat explanation. As Doris Day might have said… 'Move over, Darwin'."

"Thanks again. Creative support always welcome."

"That might imply insecurity — needing confirmation and positive feedback. Don't read too much into this but got to leave you now. I need to go."

Day 19

4.8 degrees North, 49.3 degrees West

Total nautical miles travelled by midday — 6,289

The day started sunny as they paralleled the coast of Brazil, passing about a hundred miles to the east of the mouth of the Amazon evident from the water patterns from mixing muddy freshwater with seawater. Then the rain and cloud descended, and they sailed through a grey mist for hours. It was hot and humid, like a very large sauna, considerably less expensive than the health spa on board, although not as attractive.

The elasticated waistband was starting to give him some problems. His personal one, not the one in his casual trousers — his own actual waist had increased in size, which had become noticeable when dressing in his shorts, slacks and formal trousers. He decided to limit his food intake.

He had never had that problem when he worked on the cruise liners but that may have been because he was younger, and his job had involved lots of physical activity.

Although he was not a trained dancer, he had found it was easy to learn the basics of ballroom at the dance school and he had quickly become proficient at the waltz, quickstep, foxtrot, rumba, samba, and jive. On-the-job practice linked to his natural sense of rhythm meant that he was soon recognised as a good dance partner. He could also hold a sensible conversation. Together with his sense of fun and good humour this made him attractive in the eyes of the older lady passengers on board. This was after all one of the reasons he had been hired. Client satisfaction ensured returning guests for a cruise line.

On his current cruise Burns night was celebrated with a piper, and with haggis as a starter choice. Tonight, as they headed south-eastward, they lost an hour.

Day 20

0.4 degrees North, 44.3 degrees West

Total nautical miles travelled by midday — 6,722

More rain and low cloud as they approached the equator where seemingly things are equal, hence the name. But all things never are. Day and night were pretty much the same duration all year, the distance from north to south poles was the same, and the sea temperature and air temperature were equal at around 28 degrees Celsius. The globe spun fastest here so that sunrise and sunset were the quickest. The earth here was also the fattest and, it was said, water draining from a sink would rotate in the opposite direction as the equator was crossed. Unfortunately, he could not conduct his own experiment as the bathroom sink was very small, the boat was rocking, and he was unable to persuade the commodore to stop for a few moments on the actual line for his experiment.

There was a Crossing the Line ceremony in the afternoon to initiate those who had not crossed the equator previously. Their status would improve from Pollywog (those who had not crossed) to Shellback (those who had). King Neptune presided and all were found guilty, covered in slime, and then washed off in one of the pools. A sudden squall with lashing rain ensured that most spectators also got drenched. King Neptune, surprisingly, also sought shelter from the wet.

Returning to his cabin, he found a bulletin about safety ashore in Brazil, in preparedness for the next day landing. It was headed 'Important Travel Advisory' and recommended avoiding carrying expensive items and 'anything that might easily identify you as a tourist.' He would be stepping ashore in a country peopled by generally darker skinned locals with dark hair who spoke Portuguese. He knew that he would not easily be spotted because he was an almost bald, silver haired, blue eyed, fair skinned man who spoke English.

Who would ever suspect that he and the thousand plus people getting off a newly arrived boat were tourists?

Day 21

3.4 degrees South, 38.2 degrees West

Total nautical miles travelled by midday — 7,141

It was his first time in the Southern Hemisphere on a boat. They docked in Fortaleza, Brazil, early morning, a city of high-rise apartments and hotels along the beach between the port and the old town, and his first steps in South America.

The central market was a strange concrete building constructed as a series of ramps and walkways with stalls, and a roof overhead. Definitely the best place to put a roof.

Having looked around and walked to the cathedral he took a cab with friends from the boat to see an ornate theatre inaugurated in 1910 with much decorative ironwork imported from Scotland and an elegant painted ceiling. Parts of the city were decidedly poor and the news that night reported a gangland shooting of fourteen people in a nightclub.

It was not the most attractive city and many people found it too much of a culture shock.

The weather was mild, but the intensity of the rain increased and precipitated their return to the boat.

"Very clever that — rain — precipitated/ precipitation… nice."

"And I thought you'd gone."

"Not a chance. But I'm off now. Bye!"

They sailed late afternoon, leaving so quietly and smoothly that he was only aware when he looked out of the cabin window that they were on the move again.

Day 22

7.7 degrees South, 34.5 degrees West

Total nautical miles travelled by midday — 7,525

As he awoke, he could see the distant coast of Brazil from the cabin. It varied from cliffs to lengths of high-rise buildings. They had passed the furthest easterly point of the country, the big bulge on the map of South America, and they would soon pass Recife as they started to head southwest towards their next port — Salvador.

The sky was clearer, it was dry, and the sea was calmer.

After so much time on the voyage as a passenger rather than as ship's company, he was learning the rules of onboard traveller behaviour as observed from the small number who created so much impact. If everyone could adopt these behaviours then travelling could be a dream, but not necessarily a good one. He summarised these as follows in the hope that they might be adopted and published somewhere as guidance for people planning to go on their first cruise:

Courtesy — try not to show courtesy, push between people in queues and generally do your best to ignore people. Treat members of the crew with disdain, be rude and if you need to speak, talk down to them, particularly waiters, waitresses and chambermaids. Remember the guidance you received as a child never to talk to strangers. For the avoidance of doubt speak to no one.

Corridors and other confined spaces — see Courtesy above and be certain to block the way for other people as often as possible. This works particularly well if you have a walking frame or stick and can ensure that you always walk alongside somebody who is equally as slow. When this is not possible, do your best to make others move out of the way as you barge past. And don't say 'thank you'. Be sure when passing to bump into people. This is extremely easy to do when the ship is tackling rough seas but, with enough practice, it can also be done even in a flat calm or in port.

Whenever you can, stop dead in your tracks without warning. This can make people drop their dinner or drink to the great amusement of other passengers. Again, never apologise as it is always the fault of the other person. And finally, put your feet up on furniture — that shows true breeding.

Lifts and stairways — see Courtesy and Corridors above, and be conscious of people getting in or out of the lift, or ascending or descending the stairs. Remember that your sole purpose in life is to stop them. Stand firm, if possible in groups, so as to create a barrier immediately outside the lift doors or on the top step of the stairways. If you are staying in the lift remember that the people behind you may be wanting to get off, so on no account move out of the way.

Dining — see all of the above, plus in the buffet be sure to claim your seats before you go to get food. That will stop anyone with food from sitting down to eat. If someone has left their seat, for example, to get a drink or dessert, be sure to take that seat so that they have to start over to find somewhere to consume it. Be absolutely certain to claim a window seat to see the ocean. Remember that the ship is surrounded by water and has many decks so that the restaurant seat may be one of the very few places on the entire voyage where you will be able to see the sea. And finally, when you have a seat, don't move after you have finished your meal, just sit back looking smug, dumb, disinterested or any combination of those. Should you be on the receiving end of this behaviour ask the question 'Are you getting off at, for example, Rio de Janeiro?' If the response is positive, ask if you can have the seat when they disembark.

Clothing — despite the requirement for gentlemen to wear a jacket after six p.m. ignore this petty rule and dress as if you were gardening. For both ladies and gentlemen, bring along a wide selection of bargain clothes from charity shops. If you have dressed smartly, do your best to ignore the lower life forms doing this and continue as Courtesy above.

It was sad to witness the relatively few people who could cause so much negative impact and he was not alone in wondering where the people lived and how they behaved in ordinary life.

"Are you, maybe, at risk of sounding snobbish?"

"I actually don't really care what these people think."

"Hah... maybe just proved my point. Bye for now."

Day 23

12.5 degrees South, 38.3 degrees West

Total nautical miles travelled by midday — 7,942

They docked in the early morning sunshine in Salvador, the third largest city in Brazil. Coming into port, he could see apartment blocks along miles of the coast.

He went ashore to explore the old town, on a higher level and so approached by a lift. There he found a charming assortment of houses, churches, shops and museums, many painted in pastel shades. Large amounts of renovation were in evidence as much was still in some state of decay, although this added to the charm of the area. The people were friendly and helpful, and he enjoyed a beer in a balcony bar overlooking the port and the bay. The African roots were clearly identifiable in the clothes of some of the ladies, and the artefacts for sale in many of the little shops. He liked this place a lot and could have spent more time there. It felt comfortable and safe.

The planned return was via the funicular railway, but it occurred to him that he wasn't sure if he had the inclination to do that.

"That's very subtle — inclination — funicular railway — I like that."

"Thanks for the feedback."

"My pleasure. I always level with you. Sorry, couldn't help that — inclination — level — must go."

They sailed away late afternoon.

Day 24

18.5 degrees South, 38.5 degrees West

Total nautical miles travelled by midday — 8,280

Today was a sea day, a chance to laze and doze as well as attending lectures and talking to other passengers.

Four men came through his room early to gain access to his and other balconies, and carrying buckets, paint and brushes to get rid of some of the small spots of rust caused by the constant sea spray. There must always be something to do to keep everything shipshape, he thought.

After lunch, he watched large, elegant white and black birds flying alongside and sometimes diving into the sea to catch fish near the surface, which had definitely learnt nothing from Darwin. The birds flew in great arcing circles from the bow towards the back and then glided level with the balcony along what they possibly perceived as a large moving sea cliff, using the lift created by the air pushed aside by the speeding vessel. He wondered where they lived and how they found the boat so far from land. He hoped they would not try to nest in his cabin.

He could not recall when he had started seriously to consider the meaning and purpose of life. As a small child he had played Cowboys and Indians with friends, shooting each other and falling 'dead' to the ground from imagined horses. But they had always got up. It was not a reality then.

Nor did it become a reality when older relatives died. In fact, strangely, he gave it little thought at the time. He was sad because they were no longer there in the same way as being sad when a pet died.

Sometime later in life a reality set in. He had heard a Portuguese lady once say that we are all prisoners on the planet. She had sailed the Atlantic in a small yacht with her husband and child because she wished to see more of the world.

He recognised that the only way out is clearly marked with a very large sign we all choose to ignore. Unless you opt for suicide from which statistically, we apparently have a greater probability of dying than from an accident. He had tried it twice when things had not been too good, but he just wasn't any good at it and so had failed, given up on the idea, and learned to get on with living. Failed suicides get to live to tell the tale. 'Life is short' was an expression he had heard often but nobody ever said 'death is long', although this was equally true.

Now, if he lost his sense of humour or his perspective on life, he had decided that he would turn up at a local police station to report the loss. In reality, he didn't expect a good reception or any real help, but he knew that the diversion and confusion would buy him time to recover. He might also put a small advertisement in a local paper offering a reward for its recovery as with a lost cat. And he knew that the odds of finding his missing humour were far better than of finding a furry lost animal alive. He'd seen too many small dead creatures by the roadside, never to return to their homes, but had never seen the mangled body of an emotion there.

It was impossible to take life too seriously. He wasn't alone in losing things he held dear and loved beyond measure. The death of his young son many years ago had marked him and he acknowledged that. Why would it not have, and everyone who had also known and loved him? A presence in this world had been removed against the will of everyone attached to him, and his son sure as hell would not have wished the illness or early exit from life.

He could have no belief in anything other than randomness. No gods, natural forces or science could offer any better explanation. His view was simply that we live in a very strange system. Bits of stardust that return to be the same when our living atoms become unstuck and dissolve, no longer held together by the force of life.

As he'd seen as graffiti way back in time — 'There is no gravity. The earth sucks.' Perhaps life has to suck sometimes to hold our atoms together.

He knew that death was and is a complete waste of life. To repeat, life is short — but eternity is one hell (or heaven) of a long time with more zeros on the number for infinity than the number of atoms that exist in the entire universe.

Maybe there is life after death and, if so, it must be paradise beyond our wildest imaginings because nobody ever bothers to come back.

Whatever the truth, to him the equation seemed to be completely unbalanced — how did it work, to exchange at the most say one hundred years of living for an eternity of being very dead? It didn't stack for him as a fair equation, less so because his life was now so privileged and happy.

Perhaps in the Middle Ages or in certain cultures with harsh living and few pleasures this 'deal' could be easily sold if the eternity meant paradise? He suspected no longer. It had been a pack of lies, in his opinion. Was there such a thing as a half-pack of lies he wondered? What a wonderful summing up in a court — "You have repeatedly told this court a half-pack of lies and therefore in finding you half-guilty, I sentence you to half-death. You will be hanged by the neck until half alive. May God have mercy on half your soul."

When all was said and done (as he knew one day it would be) death is simply nature's way of telling you to slow down but without any satisfaction guaranteed money back offer. Hence the only rational thing to do is to enjoy it, and that he fully intended to continue to do.

"You sounded a little bitter there."

"Yes, I guess so — a bit, but I'll get over it, thank you."

"Don't want you losing your objectivity."

"Quite right — I'd have to leg it to the nearest police station to report that loss too."

"I'm off then as long as you're OK."

That night was the commodore's cocktail party (again) and drinks at the art gallery/shop (again), followed by a blue moon (the second full moon in a calendar month) which was also a supermoon which would seem larger and brighter as it would be at its closest point to the earth. In addition, the sun had been almost directly overhead at noon, casting no shadows and to top that there was a partial lunar eclipse.

Loaded with free bubbly and an overactive imagination, thinking of vampire myths relating to a lack of shadows, he found it very hard not to think that there was some significant message for him in all this celestial activity. Portents, and omens (or is it 'oma' in the plural?) aplenty in one day.

Perhaps, he thought, as he fell asleep, the gods might be about to smile on him again as they had done so many years before.

Day 25

22.4 degrees South, 41.5 degrees West

Total nautical miles travelled by midday — 8,695

Approaching the town of Búzios, early morning, he could see the hilly coast swathed in low cloud and a total absence of tall buildings! Instead there were houses dotted along the coast and nestling in the green hillsides. Altogether considerably less developed than the last two Brazilian ports.

They stopped in the bay near to another cruise boat and tenders were used to ferry passengers ashore. He went into the town with friends and explored on foot finally taking a trip on a covered lorry with seats to see a little of the town made popular by a visit from Brigitte Bardot in the 1960s, and of the surroundings and beaches. It was an appealing and quiet place despite the tourist invasion, with attractive shops, bars and restaurants plus many expensive houses positioned on the hills for the maximum views of the ocean and bays.

He returned to the ship to watch the tenders being winched back onboard and stowed ready for the short overnight sail to Rio de Janeiro.

Another contented night's sleep followed.

Day 26

22.5 degrees South, 43.1 degrees West

Total nautical miles travelled by midday — 8,735

The alarm woke him at five forty-five. He showered and dressed quickly to go on deck to watch the sun rise as they approached Rio de Janeiro. In the dawn light, with the full moon hiding behind cloud, he saw the mountain skyline just beyond the city, very much as he expected having seen so many pictures. But it was still amazing to see as the view changed constantly with the ship's progress to the berth and the increasing daylight.

In his life he had experienced several occasions when he felt as if he was observing a film and not actually there. He'd known this feeling on his first visit to New York as if his subconscious was telling him he was imagining it all. It was happening again.

As they slowed, a number of black frigate birds glided effortlessly above the rear deck as if in a graceful welcome for the boat.

He went ashore as soon as he was permitted and caught an arranged shuttle bus to Copacabana beach which was totally in keeping with all the tourist brochure views — long, sandy and very busy. Then a taxi to a shopping mall in Barra to purchase a phone to replace one that had broken a few days prior, and then back. This gave him a good view of more of the city and of the lush tropical greenery draped all around it and on the nearby mountains. Rio was elegant and wealthy in parts with interesting architecture reminding him of Paris or Madrid, but also with incredible poverty in the Favelas he saw in the distance, and violence in several places according to his drivers.

The Portuguese had apparently discovered a large bay in January 1506 and thinking it was a river estuary had named it Rio de Janeiro meaning River of January. They did not change the name even after their mistake was realised and so Rio remains as the name.

The boat was staying in port overnight and he returned for dinner and sleep.

"You just can't get that Barry Manilow 'Copacabana' song out of your head, can you?"

"No, even though it was about a nightclub named after the beach."

"Perhaps the message not to fall in love has lodged in your subconscious?"

"I thought you were my subconscious?"

"Maybe something like that… spirit guide…? mentor? But no time for idle chatter, I'll leave you pondering. Adios!"

Day 27

22.5 degrees South, 43.1 degrees West

Total nautical miles travelled by midday — 8,735 (no change as berthed overnight)

He rose early to catch a tour bus. It soon became clear that he owed the Portuguese navigators an apology because the story of how they had named Rio was probably incorrect. Why would experienced seafarers, mistake a salty bay for a freshwater river? The tour guide outlined the current thinking. Either they had named it 'Ria', apparently the old Portuguese word for bay which had become corrupted, or it was named after a small river draining into the bay and which would have provided a welcome supply of fresh water. Bottled water would doubtless have been very difficult to obtain and just as expensive back then.

They drove past various sights and beaches with visits to the statue of Christ the Redeemer by cog-train and to the Sugar Loaf by two cable cars. In both cases he had to overcome his irrational but real fear of heights and on the first visit he scuttled from the train until he was on level ground. An appropriate posture on Corcovado (Hunchback) Mountain. The views were stunning until cloud rose from the valley to obscure the giant statue.

Before the boat sailed, he sat watching frigate birds circling above the port buildings, and while tracking a flight of ducks through binoculars he saw, in the evening light, two small kites flying.

They were heart-shaped, one blue and one pink, and he scanned the port area to see if he could find who was controlling them. After some time, he saw on the flat roof of a Favela building six stories high and with no protecting wall or balcony, that there was a white-shirted boy flying the blue kite in the fading dusk light, tugging at the string attached to the kite. It danced and fluttered above the buildings, seeming sometimes to brush past and caress the other kite as the clouds became grey, tinged with deepening pink, orange, and gold in the darkening sunset.

Before complete darkness fell, he found the other person, one floor higher and two buildings back, controlling the movements of the pink kite in a dance with the other kite. It was a young girl in a simple plain dress. The simplicity and innocence of the scene was beyond words.

Whether they knew each other, were lovers or total strangers he would never know but the joy and intimacy of the unexpected sighting moved him deeply and brought a lump to his throat.

By complete chance he had witnessed something quite magical and emotional. Something rich beyond wealth in a poor area of a city that had enthralled him. It was at times like this that he felt truly blessed. He wished them everything good in their lives and thanked them silently for him being able to share their moments. He doubted that anyone else had witnessed this and that made the experience even more significant.

Was this perhaps another sign of something to come he wondered?

Day 28

26.1 degrees South, 45.7 degrees West

Total nautical miles travelled by midday — 8,977

Sailing away in darkness from Rio the previous night, the low cloud hung over the mountains reflecting the bright lights of the city. Christ the Redeemer was illuminated rising from the haze of the cloud and creating a ghostly apparition above the darkness of the mountain backdrop.

Somehow, it was a fitting farewell.

He had watched into the early hours as the lights receded before going to bed.

When he woke, he spent a quiet morning and around noon they passed through the Tropic of Capricorn on their southward journey for two days to Uruguay and the port of Montevideo. The sea was gentle with long following waves, the sun shone, and the breeze freshened slightly.

Again, the enormity of the oceans struck him, this time the South Atlantic where they had been for some time since leaving the Caribbean. Other than the occasional ship or drilling platform there was nothing. Land was over the horizon, but he saw no fish, dolphins or whales leading him to conclude that the seas were not overpopulated.

There might well be plenty of room should humans wish to go back to aquatic living sometime.

Day 29

32.0 degrees South, 51.0 degrees West

Total nautical miles travelled by midday — 9,191

At dinner recently a supposedly reliable source had told him that on the first one third of the voyage, nine people had died. This was not a reflection on the food or the boat but just a reality of cruising in retirement years. Other guests had said they had been on a world cruise with a lady whose husband had died early on. She had arranged his cremation and continued her voyage. Difficult really to challenge the logic of that if one could remove all emotion from the event.

He understood that there were no refunds. Projecting from the current figure, twenty-seven people would be likely to die in total, say around 1.5% of the 1,700 passengers. He could understand the no refund policy as, unlike a hotel room, it would be very difficult to let out a room mid-ocean, and even harder to let out one bed or a shared bed in a room now occupied by a grieving widow or widower.

There would be a saving to the cruise line on food, but there would be the loss of revenue on drinks, probably about break-even depending upon the deceased individual's alcohol consumption and which priced beverages they had been drinking. A win/win equation… or more probably lose/lose.

Whatever, he was most definitely not going to be featuring in those statistics.

Being mid-ocean again his thoughts wandered to another scientific mystery. He was trying to understand rainfall. In theory the oceans evaporated with the heat of the sun and formed clouds, which then produced rain as they cooled and the water vapour condensed. He had learned that at school and so far, so good.

Except not. His experience told him that water turned to steam at 100 degrees Celsius and he witnessed that every time he boiled a kettle. The air temperature here was at best 30-plus degrees Celsius with a similar sea temperature. That was a big difference from 100 degrees. He also knew that the boiling point of water reduces with the increase in altitude above sea level at a rate of 1 degree Celsius of temperature reduction for approximately every 300 metres of height increase.

So, roughly 70 degrees Celsius being the difference between 30 and 100 degrees. At 1 degree per 300 metres this equates to a requirement of 21,000 metres of extra height. He didn't know of any mountains 21 kilometres high, but it would certainly explain why there are no tea shops on the top of Everest and other big lumps of upheaved rock.

It was also obvious that the boat was not 21 kilometres above sea level — the term 'sea level' means exactly that. Although it would give new meaning to the expression 'sailing the high seas'.

He knew also that some seas are at different levels and change height with sometimes very big tides but these amount to only about 10 metres, and he thought also about how heavy water is. He had carried many buckets and watering cans full of water and they were seriously heavy. If the clouds carried enormous quantities of rain why were they not so heavy that they just crashed into the ground with a big splash?

In addition, none of this supposed ocean height difference was mentioned in the voyage itinerary or during the commodore's daily announcements.

There was to his mind only one possible explanation — the theory of rainfall resulting from evaporation was rubbish. But perhaps his explanation was in some way deeply flawed and his theories were just wrong? It troubled him.

"Yes, definitely a troubled mind."

"Then by definition, for you too! Please go away, I'm busy."

"If you'd had a decent education, you'd probably be able to deal with all this stuff."

"OK, I'll apply to a university as a mature student. I have time on my hands and could do with challenging my grey matter again. Plus, having some serious time to devote to drinking would be good. And I might find a young female student who would value the company of a mature relatively wealthy man."

"Typically flippant if I may so observe. No time now to debate this any further, I have to go. See you!"

Day 30

34.5 degrees South, 56.1 degrees West

Total nautical miles travelled by midday — 9,505

Montevideo emerged from the dawn light, and they docked early morning.

On the quayside he negotiated a good US dollar price with a minibus company for a city tour without realising that the driver had lost her voice and could not give a running commentary. Not that it was terribly important given that she spoke very little English. To compound the issue the other travellers were Polish, also with limited English. He hadn't the will to renegotiate the cost.

All in all, it was an interesting three hours but he managed to understand enough as he saw the city. His view was of a city with a rich architectural heritage, much of it European influenced and art deco styled but very attractive with expanses of parkland, green roadsides, and many trees. High rises were notable by their absence until the beachside promenades on the wide expanse of the River Plate estuary which was obviously a prime real estate location.

He learned that more than half the population of Uruguay lives in the capital Montevideo and that the country is the second smallest in South America, the actual smallest one being even smaller. The name of Montevideo was said to come from the first Portuguese sailors who, on seeing the small hill behind the port area, exclaimed 'Monte veju eu' — 'I see a mountain'. Given that the hill is only about 135 metres high and would hardly count as a mountain to seasoned navigators, the word 'bollocks' sprang to his mind.

Leaving the bus, he walked through the charming old town with a carnival museum and an old market hall given over to food establishments where he sampled a local beer named Patricia and a red wine made from two local grape varieties, one of which he had not heard of. And which he forgot the name of after two thirds of a litre of alcoholic Patricia and the very generous large glass of vino tinto.

Travel broadens the mind but can also severely damage it with excessive alcohol, he concluded.

Day 31

34.3 degrees South, 58.2 degrees West

Total nautical miles travelled by midday — 9,636

A short overnight sail brought them to Buenos Aries, so named by original mariners because of the good wind that brought them there. But not before they had retraced part of their river route into Montevideo, in effect going the wrong way until they could pick up the dredged channel to Buenos Aries. It was one of his life observations played out — sometimes you have to go backwards to go forward.

The River Plate is the widest river in the world, and Buenos Aries as capital of Argentina sits on the southern side. It boasts the widest avenue in the world, tree-lined and grand with a definitely European feel to the city. French style neo-classical architecture abounds, and he was reminded by some buildings of the style of the house in the film *Psycho* but on a much larger scale and without the sinister music.

He took an open-topped bus tour to familiarise himself with the city and discovered slum dwellings, literally on the wrong side of the rail tracks from rich high-rise apartments. The city had much greenery in the trees, parks and squares with great evidence of affluence. So much affluence in fact that he saw a large dump for damaged giant rubbish bins of the type used by refuse collection lorries. He wondered if they would be recycled.

The evening was filled with a hugely professional tango show at which he was dragged by an attractive female dancer to tango with her and other equally inept members of the audience. She was a delight, but he knew her choice of him as a dancing partner was not for his looks or charm but because he was sitting at the end of a table and easy to lure onto stage. Reality check completed.

He slept well and happily after much local red wine.

Day 32

34.3 degrees South, 58.2 degrees West

Total nautical miles travelled by midday — 9,636 (no change as berthed overnight)

He went into town to the opera house, Teatro Colon, a grand building with amazing acoustics and where he was invited to sing.

Not invited to sing in the sense of being invited from the global community of opera singers to appear in an opera production, the invitation was a question from the guide as to whether anyone wanted to sing. He took the opportunity. He had now sung in the same opera house as Pavarotti and other world-class singers, admittedly to a smaller audience who had not queued for expensive tickets, and for far less time than the famous performers. Without a microphone he rendered the first line of 'My Kind of Town' and was astonished by the clarity and volume of the sound which came straight back at him in the auditorium. It was unnerving. Apparently, Pavarotti thought the place dangerous as any mistakes would be clearly heard in this theatre.

A long walk took him next to the dead centre of Buenos Aries, the Cementerio de la Recoleta. This covered thirteen acres and was the final resting place of the city's illustrious and wealthy. It was truly a city of the dead in more senses than one. The hierarchy of the ostentatious tombs indicated competition even in death, with military, naval, political, and the important, all attempting to outdo each other even in death. The poor were simply not here.

The scale and grandeur of some tombs was astonishing while others were squeezed in tight gaps between, and some were consigned to small shelves in a walled area. Many had glass fronts or doors through which the magnificent carved wooden coffins could be seen, large ornate brass handles adorning them. In extreme cases, neglect and decay over time had caused severe damage so that ceilings and parts of walls had collapsed leaving debris on the floors and often open doors where the coffins could be touched if so inclined, which he definitely was not.

Cobwebs covered the carvings of many mausolea resembling a film set for a low budget horror film, while weeds sprang from many roofs.

He was saddened to see a discarded plastic bottle in the floor rubble of one damaged tomb in which someone rested in their coffin oblivious to the decay of their once grand final home. While on an outside tomb on the fourth storey shelf, the marble front of a tomb was broken leaving a gap through which pigeons could be seen nesting alongside the coffin. He hoped that the owner was a bird lover. In some ways, new life springing from death seemed appropriate here.

There were ventilation chimneys atop many tombs, and he was baffled by them. Was it for air circulation perhaps so that the wooden coffins did not rot? He doubted it was for heating, but perhaps cooking? After all, the ancient Egyptians gave their dead items for use in the afterlife, so a barbecue and a supply of Argentinian beef to enjoy with the neighbours was a remote possibility.

It was all as if the attempts for recognition and a safe resting place after death were slowly being undone so that in due time all would return to dust and oblivion regardless of the expense of trying to avoid this. Wealth and poverty would become indistinguishable.

Where there was no evidence of any family looking after the tombs by waterproofing roofs and walls then it seemed that the small band of cemetery workers would carry the can for those who had kicked the bucket. The tools he saw being used included some handmade ladders nailed together unevenly from old timbers, the source of which he dared not contemplate, together with antique looking trailing electric cables plugged together many times in extreme lengths. They were a risk to life but, he supposed, it was a convenient place to die if fate dealt that hand.

"Oh, I like those descriptions. Very good."

"I was seriously thinking you might have gone away."

"It doesn't work like that. Gone but not forgotten as it were. Got to fly, things to do. Bye for now."

Day 33

35.8 degrees South, 55.4 degrees West

Total nautical miles travelled by midday — 9,799

It took until lunchtime to exit the River Plate and the lengthy narrow dredged shipping channel was so shallow that there was apparently very little water beneath the hull. The translation of the name of this stretch of water, Rio de la Plata, was Silver River, but the actual colour was brown from the quantities of mud and silt carried in the current.

They passed Montevideo on the horizon to the left before eventually turning southward in the sun and pleasant breeze.

With little to do he knocked around a few golf balls in a netted area on deck, chatted with people and enjoyed the sun knowing that it would soon become cooler. As he strolled around the top deck there was a pigeon perched on a rail below the funnel. It was a long way from shore, and he hoped it would get back safely to land and perhaps to its friends and family living in the tomb in Buenos Aries.

That evening from the balcony he saw an approaching bank of cloud. It was sinister — a rolling rounded wall of greyish white for as far as the eye could see, with a distinct flat top and level base under which they were about to sail. The sun disappeared as the ship entered the tunnel between the sea and the sky and with lightning flashing on distant clouds.

The storm lasted for hours, illuminating the sky and sea and with glaring sudden flashes of forked lightning searing the horizon. The temperature dropped and rain came as the wind freshened and the sea became rougher.

He sincerely hoped this was not a bad omen, but he thought that ancient sailors could easily have believed it to be so.

In the event he was to put this to the test sometime later in the voyage.

Day 34

40.6 degrees South, 60.3 degrees West

Total nautical miles travelled by midday — 10,222

Another sea day with increasing seas now classed as 'rough' and strong winds but sunny with falling temperatures. He attended two lectures, one about science and genetics, and the other about oceans and sea life.

He was surprised to learn that most of the planet's oxygen comes from plankton (between 50% and 80% varying with seasons, location etc.) rather than from rainforests at around 20%. Clearly not only should we be concerned about deforestation but also about the health of our oceans. On a personal level, he liked breathing oxygen. There didn't seem to be any alternative and only organisms living in the deepest parts of the ocean managed without it.

He knew how little time man had lived on the earth and how much more successful had been the reign of dinosaurs, but he did not know that sharks had lasted considerably longer and were still around. Perhaps crawling out of the oceans was not the brightest idea in evolution.

In terms of genetics, the prospect of growing replacement organs was mentioned together with the dangers of unintended consequences from genetic manipulation. He'd have to leave all that to the scientists — it was way beyond his sphere of knowledge but the occasional replacement bit might come in useful as he got older.

Tomorrow would bring landfall in an area where whales visited each year from June to December, but this being February they would be somewhere else and so there was no chance of a sighting. In September and October, they could be seen with their young, and diving tours plus boat trips to observe them were available, creating a part of the local tourism income.

"How would humans feel if coachloads of small mammals kept popping in to local maternity wards to watch?"

"Good point. But probably unlikely. Are you back now?"

"Yes, but only until something more interesting comes up."

Day 35

42.4 degrees South, 65.1 degrees West

Total nautical miles travelled by midday — 10,484

He went ashore in Puerto Madryn, Patagonia, and was glad to be wearing jeans, socks and a sweater as the wind was biting. This was summer here so he tried to imagine what winter would be like. Welsh settlers had landed in 1865 and the language was still in use in the general area although diminishing. The local Indians had apparently aided the settlers, a complete reversal of behaviour from other colonised areas on his trip.

The Indian heritage was apparent in the appearance of some of the local peoples and he wondered what had drawn the Welsh and other settlers from Spain and Italy etc. to leave the familiarity of their homelands for completely unknown new places. Things must have been very bad at home, but they must also have had painted a very rosy picture of the prospects in the new land. Were they, he wondered, disillusioned and downhearted when first they landed in a bleak and cold country?

The bigger question remained as to why humans had left the middle of Africa to venture to other parts, and how did they get there? In Africa they would have survived easily grazing on berries and eating the occasional antelope or similar so why trek, ride or sail to somewhere new and have to invent warm clothing and agriculture to get by? Travel agents back then must have been extremely persuasive and truth in advertising was clearly a concept for future generations. It was a pity that no brochures remained to tell the story.

Puerto Madryn was small and tidy and contained shops and stores appropriate to a working town, but there was little to excite a visitor. It was unlike the Caribbean ports he had been used to visiting when he worked on the cruise liners.

Back then, the time ashore was an opportunity to catch the sun on a beach or to shop in the colourful towns. Colourful due to both the painted houses in so many pastel shades but also from the colourful personalities of the local people, and their obvious love of living. There was sometimes an edge to these places, particularly off the beaten track, but as a fairly frequent visitor he got to know his way around many ports and to be recognised in some.

It was often an opportunity to visit a bank to top up his savings. His earnings as entertainment crew were paid in US dollars and he was able to save because his board and keep onboard were provided. Drink was at a discounted crew rate compared to guest prices and he usually drank from bottles purchased ashore and kept in his shared cabin. But the bulk of his income came as a result of a stroke of luck and an imaginative and creative mind.

In turn, and over a number of years, his savings built up and he purchased properties from which he earned rental income. Life was going well until a considerable amount of his money vanished, disappeared, or evaporated depending on which description felt least bad, when Chartered Caribbean Bank closed its doors.

To be precise, its doors were closed for it by the bank regulator when the chief executive was found to be guilty of fraud, corruption, mismanagement, incompetence, false accounting, trading insolvently, lying, market manipulation, insider trading, and womanising. All of this was in addition to some unsavoury activities he had indulged in. In those times, involvement in a reasonable number of these behaviours might have been completely acceptable, but he had gone for broke and perhaps unexpectedly to him, achieved precisely that. So much so that even the backhanders allegedly paid to the authorities could not prevent him being made an example of.

The lavish parties held regularly by the bank had been attended by local dignitaries, business people, clients and their partners (lavishly and expensively dressed) and attractive young ladies (often somewhat underdressed but doubtless this was due to their lack of education in how to dress and behave at a dinner party and the fact that they had generally not been to finishing school). With expensive caterers and wine merchants supplying other delights for the attendees these were apparently events not to be missed. But all of this great number of dignitaries, politicians, lawyers and other members of the communities eventually lost money together with their prime source of entertainment.

It must have been hard for them to readjust and he doubted that they would ever again be able to milk such generosity.

He had lost a large sum and it felt worse because he had not benefitted from even a single party invitation.

He continued to save hard for a few more years until he was forced to return to dry land and he returned to the UK to look after his properties, to explore his entrepreneurial curiosity, and to work in property sales for day-to-day income.

There he ultimately met the lady who would become his second wife and the mother of their two boys.

Back in Patagonia, they sailed again late afternoon, heading further south and west towards the pointy skeletal finger at the end of the South American continent and ultimately Cape Horn and the Pacific.

And he reflected on how early navigators sailing in minuscule ships would have fared — wet, freezing, malnourished and downright scared.

Day 36

47.1 degrees South, 64.5 degrees West

Total nautical miles travelled by midday — 10,774

Albert Ross! Albert Ross!

Could he perhaps have been the discoverer of these birds whoever he was? 18th century predictive text could then perhaps have scrambled this to arrive at the ornithological name.

Albatross.

Lots of them flying by the boat. Banking and turning in parallel to the front and then wheeling back gracefully and effortlessly to the stern and returning close to the boat or at some distance. The most effort he saw from them through the binoculars was a foot held out briefly as an airbrake to make a tight turn. Through the binoculars it was as if he was flying with them, and he could see so much detail of this beautiful bird with a wingspan of more than two metres.

He wondered how they slept so far away from the shores of either the Falkland Islands or Argentina and, as if in answer, several minutes later he spotted several of them sitting on the water in the long ocean swell whilst one of them swallowed a fish held in its beak.

It was impossible not to remember schooldays and *The Rime of the Ancient Mariner.* He could now be described as one of that breed, he guessed.

There had been dolphins last evening too, as the boat moved into open water after leaving port, and reports today of whales, which he hoped to see. All he saw in the sea were large patches of weed floating. The weather was cool but with beautiful blue skies, and the sea was no longer the blue of the tropics but more an olive green to grey colour that looked uninvitingly cold.

A quiet evening with little to do other than eat and chill in the cabin with a glass of whiskey and a film on TV before sleep.

Valentine's Day approached with nobody to give chocolates or a card to. No matter, it was what he had expected.

Day 37

52.8 degrees South, 64.8 degrees West

Total nautical miles travelled by midday — 11,115

When he awoke early, the sea was rough with white-capped waves rolling towards the boat which was pitching lightly. The progress southwards continued with no sightings of whales or anything other than birds.

And, despite the announcement from the bridge about the Albert Rosses around the ship, it turned out that they weren't that at all, they were petrels. Their beauty was undiminished but the romance of the rhyme had gone, and he couldn't think of any poems about these birds.

He attended another lecture on sea life and was reminded from his diving days how badly human ears function underwater. Sound travels very well but direction can't be detected as our ears are tuned in to sound waves travelling through the air. Not so the dolphins, porpoises and whales, the latter of which can call to other whales over hundreds of miles to say they have been delayed and will be home later. Clearly no market there for mobile phones.

Despite all the amenities on board he thought that he was becoming institutionalised and somewhat bored with the sea days. It was a different matter in the cold from cruising in the tropics with warmth and sun, and the ship felt crowded particularly at meal times because nobody was on deck or ashore.

In two days' time that would be remedied with a stop in port and he held no hope meanwhile of finding anything else to relieve the increasing boredom.

She had boarded at Buenos Aries although he did not notice her for a few days, and then only by chance. He had gone to the Commodore Club overlooking the bow on a whim after the evening show in the theatre. It was fifty/fifty if he would have a nightcap or just head to bed, but the thought of a cocktail and listening to the pianist playing and singing some of the standards that he used to perform appealed. They were some of his favourites and they often triggered warm memories.

He had known that evening that he needed to deal with the boredom, and after showering and dressing for dinner, he suddenly felt very positive about life for no obvious reason. He simply felt good, and he knew that in his dinner jacket and black tie he looked smart.

As he walked slowly in to the bar area he looked around the dimly lit room for friends to talk with but saw nobody. The venue was extremely quiet that night. He looked right towards the bar area on the raised central staging beyond the grand piano, and stopped. She was perched on a bar stool with finely shaped legs — as he would later embellish the story, hers were pretty good too, as he had been able to discern from the subtle split in her long black ball gown.

He had heard people say that their breath had been taken away by an event and for him it had just happened. He remained momentarily immobile, and he felt unable to move until something in his mind recognised how he must look, and he regained as much control as he could. He had a choice, but he also knew immediately that, in reality, he had none. If he did not make an approach this beautiful creature might be forever lost to him… and if he did make an approach the magic might dissipate in an instant; if for example she spoke badly, was dull, didn't speak English, or simply rejected him.

He moved forward. She was watching the pianist and for a second, he considered just walking past. He took a breath whilst searching for the right thing to say.

"Excuse me, but are you alone and would you mind if I join you?"

He was signalling to the adjoining bar stool as the words fell from his mouth before his mind could edit them. She gave him what he thought momentarily was a cold look and then the corner of a red lip curled almost imperceptibly before breaking into a smile.

"How very English," she said, "and to answer your questions, 'no' to both."

He detected a slight accent, certainly not South American or Spanish but something cultured and exotic, beautifully spoken, and very, very, sexy. Her response confused him, and it must have shown on his face.

"Let me clarify my answer for you," she said with a touch more accent showing, "I am here with a work colleague, and I would certainly have no objection if you wished to sit beside me, particularly as you requested this of me in such an English way. Are you a gentleman?"

"Of course," he responded, "I try always to be a gentleman in the company of a lady. But if you mean, do I have a title, or own a large country estate then no." He paused.

"May I buy you a drink?" he asked.

She ordered a martini, he a whiskey, and they talked easily. It took him only minutes to understand that he wanted her — in all the senses of the word, not simply a sexual attraction but so much more, as if such a small word as 'wanted' could contain so much. And he wanted her not just for the moment but for all his life and more. He recognised the insanity of these thoughts, but he lumbered on clear in his knowledge that a future was already written for him, if the gods truly were smiling on him. But much more importantly if they happened also to be smiling on her in the same way.

He could not help or edit the feeling, not that he wished to, but it was alien to him and stronger than the strongest feeling he'd ever had in any relationship. That truly scared him but the fear itself also became part of the indescribable emotion flowing through his veins and pulsating in his heart. Love at first sight had always been an unreal concept to him and he had always been deeply cynical when people spoke or wrote about it. So, what was it that was happening to him? And how much he feared that it might not be reciprocated.

He focussed on the conversation but was drawn into her eyes and he felt his thoughts swimming. By some major effort he attempted to appear completely relaxed and unaffected. He was sure it showed.

She was from Denmark and worked occasionally in film, theatre and television. She had been a presenter years back of a children's television show that had been popular in its time and since then she had moved on to more serious acting. Her visit to Buenos Aries was to explore with a TV producer a small series of films focussed on single ladies of a certain age travelling independently to exotic places, and of the risks and rewards of doing this. They would be low budget, sponsored and with a market for the non-mainstream alternative TV channels plus, perhaps, planes and cruise companies.

Her accent was slight but totally captivating, and she was both eloquent and elegant — tall, slim, with long blonde hair and totally beautiful to his eye.

They re-ordered drinks twice, and talked animatedly about everything, enjoying the exchange of ideas, knowledge, and each other. She had never married but had been in one long relationship that it seemed had simply run its course. He told her about his life. They were similarly aged, and he told her how much younger he had thought she was on first seeing her. She responded similarly and they thanked each other for the compliment promising to exchange used non-sequentially numbered bank notes in plain envelopes as payment for their respective compliments. She shared his humour and laughed easily with him.

In the early morning hours, they concluded that it was time to get some sleep. He helped her down from the bar stool, and unexpectedly, she linked arms with him as they walked from the bar towards the lifts. It was not as he momentarily thought just for balance on the moving boat.

She stopped and turned towards him. Before he could think, he gently pulled her towards him and kissed her.

She pulled back and the look in her eyes was unreadable. He feared that he had destroyed everything by acting so impulsively. Her gaze went into his soul. He had no other description for it. It penetrated him deeply. His heart pounded even more, and he was about to apologise and leave when she took his hand to her cheek, and leaned in to kiss him slowly, passionately, and tenderly for a lingering fraction of eternity.

"I want you," she said softly.

He had been both mesmerised and confused and had spoken in absolute truth what he thought. "I don't usually do this on a first date."

It sounded, he thought, stupid but it was sincere and was meant to say so much about his feelings for her. He realised too that he may have interpreted her words wrongly. Perhaps it had not been meant as an invitation.

"And I never do this," she had said taking his hand and leading him to the staircase where they descended one floor and walked the brief distance to her cabin. They entered in semi-darkness; the room illuminated only by the light of the moon. As they held each other they kissed gently.

"You do realise," he whispered, "that this is insane."

"Yes," she said, "a delicious insanity between two crazy people, but I know it is right for me and I want to pursue it wherever it takes me."

"Even to the moon?" he asked quietly teasing and stroking her hair.

"Especially to the moon," was her almost breathless answer.

They did not undress fully. She turned away from him and he unzipped her long dress and helped her from it. She helped him to undress partially and for some strange reason they both placed their clothes carefully over the back of a shadowy chair and in the dim light, looked slowly into each other's eyes.

They climbed into her bed and held each other while some process of blending or merging took place and they both joined in some magical way by merely holding, stroking and kissing. And then they fell asleep in each other's arms as the process continued through the night hours. There was no sex.

It would have been, in some odd way, an irrelevance.

Day 38

54.4 degrees South, 68.1 degrees West

Total nautical miles travelled by midday — 11,307

When he woke, she was propped on one elbow looking at him and smiling. It was early and they were docked in Ushuaia.

"If you thought last night was crazy, try this," she said slowly, "I think I could be in danger of falling in love with you. I'm not accustomed to such feelings, but it seems as though I have already known you forever."

He paused briefly. "I know. We've been together somewhere before this. But I can't explain it, or how I know it… or even if it is true. But I believe it with every part of my being. And I thank the gods for allowing us to meet."

They kissed and she folded into his arms while their bodies spoke without words.

They had both booked the same shore excursion and so eventually and reluctantly they got up. She came dripping from the shower with a towel partly around her and she stood looking at him still in bed waiting for the bathroom. Then she let the towel fall and stood smiling as he let out a sigh. Her body was, to his eyes, perfect and she stepped towards him saying flirtingly, "This is just a preview. The main feature will be later. Do you like what you see?"

"No," he replied, "I don't like it at all."

He watched her slight and brief confusion before quickly continuing, "I adore it and I want to keep looking. You are truly beautiful."

"We must save this," she said. "There are other things to see today and there will be much time later for us."

As they went ashore, he pointed out to her that they had sailed the Beagle Channel while they slept, so named after the boat on which Darwin had been a young passenger starting to observe the world and to develop his theories. He told her how relieved the Royal Geographical

Society, or whoever, must have been after a voyage lasting several weeks to receive the historic message 'The Beagle has landed'.

He was surprised that she understood him. As she said, "We too have heard of Darwin. You English are so insular."

"Comes from being an island race," he replied, and they both smiled.

Ashore, they explored Ushuaia on foot, wrapped up against the summer weather. It was cold and windy, but the small city had charm with assorted building styles from pastel coloured wooden buildings with corrugated roofs, to concrete residential and office blocks all rising up the hill from the port.

It reminded him of Iceland and her of home. They linked arms or held hands and kissed in several doorways, talking animatedly as they discovered small interesting things. They had coffee and checked their emails then returned to the pier for their coach and tour.

They were driven through town to catch a narrow-gauge railway through forests and following a river at the foot of snow-capped mountains. It had originally been a train to take prisoners to and from logging work and the description of the conditions then was saddening.

They eventually arrived at 'The End of the World' overlooking the Beagle Channel, and on the far side the mountains at the tail end of the Andes, and Chile. He told her how remarkable it was that they had literally gone to the end of the earth to find each other and that there could not have been a more appropriate way of meeting. She kissed him and he saw a small tear in her eye. Perhaps it was the cold wind, but he thought not.

They returned to the ship for the departure late afternoon to Cape Horn but not before addressing a problem of logistics. Quickly they agreed that she would change in her cabin and then she would come to spend the night with him after dinner.

He had suggested playfully that she might wish to visit him to see his etchings.

"What," she asked with a degree of suspicion, "are these 'itchings'?."

It took a little while to explain and she then laughed and kept repeating the word slowly, savouring the sound and the new knowledge.

They decided to dine at his table as there was a spare place and she thought the company at her table uninteresting other than her business companion who understood and was happy for her. His dining colleagues welcomed her as he knew they would, and he sensed their pleasure in seeing him with such a delightful and animated partner.

Their first hours together had stolen the day, and eventually another dusk descended. Against the late sunset they went to his cabin and made slow love to and with each other until there was nothing more except the most natural sleep entwined, interlocked, satiated and enthralled.

And, without question, each of their gods somewhere was smiling in satisfaction.

Day 39

55.5 degrees South, 67.1 degrees West

Total nautical miles travelled by midday — 11,459

They woke to loudspeaker announcements of the arrival at Cape Horn, in the Southern Ocean, famed for ferocious sea conditions. This was the furthest south that either of them had been. Not surprising, given that Antarctica was the next land, but odd because 55.5 degrees South was only equal in northern hemisphere latitudes to the top of Scotland and her home town of Copenhagen.

They watched through the balcony window as the cloud briefly broke to reveal the sight of a bleak desolate alien landscape, with sunshine for minutes only, heavy dark seas, sleet, and vicious winds.

A photographer was sent ashore, but the inflatable craft got into difficulties returning, and there ensued a long fight to get that boat and two rescue craft back in increasing seas and wind. They watched anxiously, huddled together on a wind-scoured open deck moving in every direction and at an extreme angle. Eventually, the rescue was completed, and the ship sailed in violent winds with a list that seemed severe and made moving around the cabin difficult. They retreated to the bed because they agreed that would make everything much safer, and they ordered a room service lunch plus champagne.

It was Valentine's Day and they had both forgotten until he found an advertising flyer under the door. He modified the blank reverse side as a card and gave her several small chocolates saved from the ones left each night on his pillow by his cabin stewardess, together with a promise always to remember from now on. Her apology and gift were several gentle kisses.

Room service seemed to have a little difficulty understanding the request for two lunches in a cabin with one occupant but they both thought this could not have been the first onboard romance they'd encountered.

They ate lightly and drank champagne toasting every possible thing they could think of that they were grateful for. Then, with the rocking and swaying of the boat they made sensuous slow love until they drifted into satisfied sleep, holding each other closely and fondly like one entity.

They had exchanged a great amount of detail about themselves on their first night and they knew that they were both without brothers or sisters. Their parents had died some years ago. He had three children and she had none. His two divorces contrasted with her single significant relationship lasting more than twenty years. Her partner had disappeared without trace (she had tried hard to locate him) and without explanation (she had tried hard to understand). She did not think he was dead as there were no reports from hospitals, police, his work colleagues, or his friends to indicate this or of someone suffering from memory loss. He had not indicated that he was unhappy and there had been no falling out. He had disappeared from the film and TV scene in which he worked without any clue as to where he'd gone. She might, therefore, never know what had happened and was resigned to that and to mourning a sort of artificial loss. She admitted when questioned that she sometimes wondered if she was somehow to blame, but that she did not believe so.

She was Sofia Larsen, born in a small village not far from Copenhagen to which she had moved for university and then work. He was Marcus Anthony, known by most people as Marc. (With that surname how could his parents have resisted the obvious Christian name?) As it happened, it was also easily remembered socially but he changed it as a stage name to Tony Marks on the basis that the Jewish implication might help in getting more work as a singer from agents. As one entertainment agent had told him, "Tony, it won't fool anyone. You're about as Jewish as a bacon baguette." Nevertheless, he worked with that name for years.

It didn't occur to him until later that as a musician he could have simply added 'lend me your ears' to his real name on publicity blurb for maximum effect. When he told her that, she understood and thought it funny, having read Shakespeare at school. In return, he could only claim to have read some Hans Christian Andersen as a small child and *Hamlet* in secondary school. He felt 'insular' for this and informed her, which

86

amused her even more. "I think I shall call you 'Insular Marc'," she said, although he told her it sounded like something to do with central heating.

It was becoming clear that they spoke the same language. Not simply a common tongue of English but a common sense of the absurd, of wordplay and of similar intellects. They played with each other both physically and in speech and were comfortable with the intimacy of shared humour which they affectionately directed at each other.

But it did not always work. She noted in his room that he too had for some reason best known to the housekeeping staff precisely seven pillows.

"My seven pillows of wisdom," he had answered nimbly not knowing how he had conjured that up. She was completely lost, and it took more explanation than the joke was worth, and more time that he would rather have spent on meaningful conversation. All he could do was apologise and kiss her. She seemed OK with that.

That afternoon they sailed the Beagle Channel spotting large numbers of penguins on passing islands. He wondered aloud why they were always dressed formally for dinner whatever the time of day. She bettered that by telling him that the word penguin derived from the Welsh — pen gwyn — white head, and that she remembered a story about a little girl in school who had to read a book about them and write an appraisal. 'This book' she had written 'told me more about penguins than I wanted to know'. He loved that.

Late afternoon they again passed Ushuaia to the starboard and entered Glacier Alley, which was beyond any expectations and beautiful almost beyond belief. The glaciers filled the valleys with blue-tinged white ice, clinging to rock faces, magnificently enormous, giving off streams and impressive waterfalls that dived into the channel. They watched through binoculars taking turns and alternating their exclamations at the wonder. As they observed the magnified images it seemed as though they were flying over the ice and rock. It was quite beautiful. The scale and number of these frozen formations was spectacular with the unrealistically jagged and sharp high peaks of the snow-covered Andes mountains looming above them, sometimes shrouded in cloud.

Before dressing for dinner, they had gin and tonic from his fridge. Playfully she asked him if he had enough ice, looking over his shoulder at the gigantic lump of it in the valley the ship was passing.

He was really taken with this lady and held her closely as he told her so.

At the formal Valentine's dinner she and all the ladies were given a single red rose which perfectly matched her beautiful evening gown. The beauty of the flower and of her personality and looks was not lost on him and quietly he gave thanks again to his gods.

"I haven't gone away but you seem to be otherwise occupied at present, so I'll say bye for now."

"Thanks, I'm fine without interruptions."

"OK, I'm off. Enjoy!"

Day 40

53.1 degrees South, 70.5 degrees West

Total nautical miles travelled by midday — 11,834

They had moved to her cabin late last night. It seemed logical and they agreed to continue to alternate between the two rooms until she left the ship in Fort Lauderdale where she was to stay for a few days of work meetings before flying home. She had previously advised her business colleague onboard that her situation had changed and that she would meet up from time to time only for any relevant business discussions.

The ship was positioned off Punta Arenas, Chile, as they awoke. The view from her cabin balcony window was of a grey low city, but they wanted to walk around to explore it and so took a tender to go ashore for a few hours.

It became clear that they both enjoyed doing their own thing more than being shepherded around and organised, with the pleasure of discovering new experiences and chance happenings. They had coffee in a small restaurant where above and behind the bench seat was written 'And in the end the love you take is equal to the love you give', a misquoted Beatles lyric. It made sense, and he related something he had read years back and believed in, that everything and everyone has a message for you if you are there long enough to hear it. It had just been evident again, but more was to come, and it was unexpectedly soon.

They got by in basic Spanish and followed directions to the cemetery to see the tombs of the wealthy local families, and of sailors who had died in the local waters. Grand mausolea again spoke of wanting to display importance even in death but in contrast there were more simple graves where brightly coloured plastic flowers were placed. The contrast between those and the grey sky and drizzle was notable.

Walking back towards the city centre, they waited for the green pedestrian crossing light allowing them to cross at a road junction. As they walked across, traffic from the adjoining road to the right started on their own green light and a large vehicle accelerated left round the corner.

He saw it coming towards them and realised that it was increasing in speed and going to hit them. The driver could not have seen them. In the smallest fraction of time he reacted, waving his arms, shouting and leaning forward to brace for impact and hoping that she was still behind him and protected by him.

The driver reacted and hit the brakes stopping as Marc's outstretched arms and his hands pushed against the car bonnet and he took a rapid step backwards. His instinctive reactions had been exactly right. She was untouched and he was unhurt. He walked to the driver who opened his window and apologised profusely. Then he smiled at the driver, said all was fine and shook his hand. His calm in that instant surprised him. It may simply have been relief at not being either dead or damaged.

Walking away he held her and checked that she was OK, and then they held each other tightly and voiced their luck for the escape. She said that she didn't want to lose him and that she had no time to react or scream, but had simply watched frozen in the split second it had taken. He told her that he wasn't that easy to get rid of and in any case, he had no desire to go back to the cemetery for a second visit.

A drink was needed and so they walked to the city square to the Hotel José Nogueira and the small, intimate Shackleton Bar they had passed earlier. They ordered two of the local cocktail, pisco sour, which they savoured, and enjoyed the panelled bar with painted ceiling, chandelier and watercolour paintings of the ill-fated Shackleton Antarctic expedition and rescue. Plus, they listened to great R&B music playing through the speakers. The scare a few minutes earlier had crystallised their certainty about their feelings and they promised to do everything they could to protect their future time together. It was too precious not to.

He commented that the bad portent earlier in the spookily eerie sky and storm after Montevideo must have been overwhelmed by the positive forces of their smiling gods. He only partly believed this, but his partial belief was matched by hers and they allowed the romanticism of their thoughts to blossom in the joy of still being together… and simply of still being.

Returning to the boat they had dinner, watched a show, and went to his cabin. Housekeeping was going to get very confused by two cabins completely unused on alternate nights. They were not however going to concern themselves too much about housekeeping.

He would find a moment tomorrow to explain to his maid.

Day 41

51.5 degrees South, 74.5 degrees West

Total nautical miles travelled by midday — 12,141

They were woken in the night by the strong movements of the ship. They had left the Magellan Straits through which the boat of navigator Ferdinand Magellan had apparently been blown by the wind to reach the relative calm of the Pacific Ocean, which he had named for that reason. That night it was not being very peaceful, but they were both good sailors and happily held tightly to each other laughing that not only had the earth moved for them, but now the ocean as well. They slept — mostly.

After breakfast they sat quietly watching the sea and then the journey away from open ocean via islands of varying sizes and narrowing channels. The hills were stark grey stone becoming increasingly wooded and green as they went further from the ocean. They had not realised how numerous the Chilean islands were as the maps they had seen at school did not show so much detail. Some small islands had navigation markers but there was no sign of habitation or of birds or wildlife. Silver streams on the rock faces flashed in the sunlight between the clouds but this was a barren unwelcoming place — a true wilderness, and the journey along these passages took many hours.

Eventually the tall spines of the snow-capped Andes appeared again, unreasonably jagged sharp peaks swathed in snow, ice and cloud dropping steeply to green tree-lined shores stretching along the coastlines for great distances.

During these quiet hours, he asked her gently what she thought had happened between them, not that he was challenging this, but out of a sense both of wonder and curiosity, he explained. She responded that she was planning to ask him a similar question. She admitted to having seen him on board before they met and found him interesting and intriguing in a way she could not rationalise. He had, she said, a presence. When he had spoken to her in the bar, she had immediately felt an affinity and overwhelming attraction that grew the more they had talked. It was inevitable that they should become lovers and there was no reason intellectually or emotionally why she should have delayed the action she took. Her conscious and unconscious mind were in agreement on this.

He listened and she then asked the same question of him. He paused only briefly before saying that it must have been fate. There was no rational explanation for the magnetic attraction, the chemistry between them, and the way he had simply fallen for her almost in an instant. He observed that each of these was a physical description that was totally inadequate because no words could adequately describe what had happened and how. He just knew that it had. And, he added that it was absolutely an act of insanity.

"There is apparently," he said, "a very fine line between genius and insanity. I just managed to rub it out."

"Well," she replied smilingly, "I have become mad for you... and I think you also for me?"

They were approaching the Amalia glacier and it was late afternoon. They saw three dolphins swimming in perfect synchronicity, each surfacing at the same instant as the others as they swam near to the boat before disappearing as rapidly as they had appeared The glacier was large and impressive but did not have the same impact as the row of glaciers they had first seen a couple of days back. The boat rotated so that everyone on board could see it properly and their attention from the balcony was caught by one small black bird sitting on a chunk of dirty ice floating near the boat. It gave some degree of perspective and reality to the whole scene and it amused them to see it bobbing along before eventually taking flight over the surface of the water.

They set off for the next destination, retracing the last part of their route. It was to be a quiet night in her cabin.

"Quite a bit there again about your subconscious I see."

"I really did think you'd gone away."

"To quote you, 'I'm not that easy to get rid of,' although that was a bit of a close call yesterday for us both!"

"Yes, it was. Maybe I can put up with you in the circumstances."

"By the way, nice lady."

"Yes, I think so."

"Correction — we both think so. Got to dash."

Day 42

49.5 degrees South, 74.2 degrees West

Total nautical miles travelled by midday — 12,265

It was a totally grey morning, cold and rainy with low cloud masking the sky and wisps of isolated lower cloud blowing along the cliff faces. They were in a tight steep fjord facing the vast Pio XI glacier with its high wide icy front descending to the water. It was blue white in places, but other parts were dirty with the rock and earth that it carried. A large number of small icebergs encircled the ship and bounced in the milky grey opaque water.

Overall, the effect was not so much of grandeur as of unearthliness — a mass of ice apparently forty-one miles long, trapped between the mountains and the cold sky. They had arrived early morning, which prompted him to ask why when the glacier had been around for thousands of years they needed to show up before the sun had even got up.

It was somewhere they were happy to leave and the views of steep cliffs dropping vertically into the water as they headed back towards the open sea were more inspiring. Trees clung impossibly to near vertical rock and innumerable waterfalls cut valleys through the rock face, some small and others colossal in scale. It was a prehistoric landscape where they would not have been surprised to see dinosaurs.

There was plenty of time to relax and to reflect on the long sail from there, and they chatted idly.

"By the way," she suddenly said, "I have some things to add to my answer yesterday. I wasn't looking for anything, I was completely content; I thought I had everything. But I was wrong. I hadn't realised that I was going without closeness, sensuality, and intimacy. Suddenly this was obvious to me — it felt right and those things I now have again are a part of all this. My seventh sense tells me."

"I like the idea of a seventh sense," he said knowing she had probably confused sixth sense with maybe seventh heaven, or his seven pillows of wisdom. But he had no need to correct her.

"I think, for me, it's like having misplaced something and not realising until suddenly you have a need to find it. Like cufflinks," he said playfully, "always turn up when you aren't looking."

"What," she asked quietly, "is this cough lynx creature?"

"We're going to have so much fun," he answered before giving her a very big kiss, explaining and continuing. But the image of the wheezing wild cats stuck with him.

"So, why did you really want me? Was it just for the desire, the lust, the physicality, the bonding, the coupling, my natural charm and the great sex… or was there maybe something more?" he asked her jokingly.

"I figured you would be cheaper than taking English lessons," she replied adopting quite unexpectedly an American accent. He laughed aloud. She both surprised and delighted him in equal measure and he was getting to like her more every minute of every day.

By late afternoon they had made open sea and the Pacific again. Predictably it was anything but calm, and the extreme winds pushed the tall boat into a strong list to port while the size and strength of the waves increased and caused the boat to move around a lot.

They dressed for the formal dinner prior to the South Pacific Ball. She had on her black evening dress and he too dressed exactly as he had when they met. They went back to the Commodore Club at the top of the ship and at the bow to see the wild sea, and then to savour a quiet gin and tonic before dinner.

They sat in a far corner for privacy, and despite the movement of the ship, he stood and sang to her quietly from the musical *South Pacific* the romantic ballad sung by the French plantation owner 'Some Enchanted Evening'. It had not before been on his list of favourite songs or in his repertoire, but it occurred to him that the location and the lyrics fitted their situation. Except that he had not first seen her across a crowded room. Substituting the word 'empty' for 'crowded' would have scanned equally well but somehow seemed disloyal to the song.

After dinner they danced in the disco atop the ship, rather than at the formal ball, and there was great amusement because the movements the ship was making made their dance moves very odd.

And then they retreated to bed to again be rocked gently to sleep.

Day 43

45.2 degrees South, 74.8 degrees West

Total nautical miles travelled by midday — 12,591

The sea remained lumpy and the pitching movement of the boat continued under grey skies punctuated by occasional outbreaks of sun. They passed some of the time on this sea day talking about their past lives, and he told her how his interest in music had initially led him into amateur operatics and several pantomimes before working on the cruise liners. He explained to her that he had acted the role of dame several times and that another song from *South Pacific* had reminded him of that, the amusing 'There is Nothing Like a Dame'.

"There is nothing like a Dane?" she asked.

"No, not Dane like you but what a lovely idea. No, dame as in woman. I used to dress as a woman on stage."

"I have seen some shows like that," she said, her face a picture. "San Francisco, I think."

"Not quite the same actually, this was pantomime."

"I have heard of that, but I don't know about it. I think it is popular at Christmas in England?" she said. "Tell me everything about this pantomime please, I would like to learn."

He explained to her about audience participation, with the shouts of, "Oh, yes, it is! Oh, no, it isn't!" and, "It's behind you." And he told her a little about the history and the watering down in recent years with minor celebrities appearing, and plots being less salacious when the original reason had been to satirise and poke fun at the establishment, hence the dim baron and often the social reversal when maid becomes princess, or poor boy finds incredible good fortune etc.

And then it got more difficult — "The prince is called principal boy and is a girl, and he/she falls in love with a beautiful girl who is a girl, from a lower social class. Her mother and possibly her sisters are men who are very ugly, and they often want to marry the prince who is a girl.

"There is a not very bright young boy, who is often an older man who has been on TV once or twice and may be a comedian or have a stuffed animal as a part of his act. And there will be a horse or donkey, or something similar which has two people in it. And an older dim man as the father of the beautiful girl.

"And finally, the 'baddie', a dark sinister creature with menace who may be played by someone gay and a little camp. This part may be interchangeable with not very bright boy. The story will be a mostly recognisable fairy-tale but modified a lot and will contain very bad jokes that are sometimes double-entendre but changed to suit the younger or older audiences between afternoon matinee and evening performances."

Her expression was blank.

"I'll take you to see one," he offered, "that might help."

"I think perhaps I will need therapy after seeing all this confused sexuality?" she asked with a broad grin.

"Possibly… very, very, possibly," he responded, "but I think I can help."

In the afternoon they watched a film in the theatre. It was still cold, grey and wet outside so there was little point in being on deck for more than a few minutes of fresh air. It turned out to be a love story, a sort of modern fairy-tale and with a theme tune 'You'll Never Know Just How Much I Love You' that his mother used to sing to him as a very small child. His new love was moved as much as him when he told her that, and how emotional it had suddenly made him to realise his mother must have been singing it to speak of her love for him.

"Ah, your ghosts again."

"Yes, but welcome ones even if sad."

"Remember to make today's emotions into future ghosts you'll be happy to meet again."

"Very philosophical, but thank you for that."

"What I'm here for… maybe… see you soon."

Day 44

41.2 degrees South, 72.5 degrees West

Total nautical miles travelled by midday — 12,881

They were anchored off Puerto Montt, Chile and the day was warmer and sunny. After breakfast they took a tender ashore to walk around the small city. There was a long promenade passing a fairground where all the rides were old and faded. It was not open, but they strolled through it and recalled times when they were young and, in each case, vividly remembered the lights, sounds and excitement of visiting fairgrounds near their homes each summer.

The town had an assortment of architecture, from modern concrete to corrugated metal buildings painted blue, and other older properties painted in pale colours. There was a large bus station and a great many backpackers who had presumably come to camp and trek in the lake area not far from the town.

Further on they entered a shopping mall and a department store. There was very little different on sale from elsewhere on their travels — the world they agreed was becoming almost the same everywhere. They doubted that they would be able to visit anywhere unspoilt. But they did see a kiosk selling herbal remedies in colourful boxes for numerous ailments. One had a quite explicit photo of a couple making love alongside cures for heart conditions, lung problems, and aches in all parts of the body. They could not translate the wording, but the illustrations were clear, and he ventured that the graphically illustrated product, because of the nature of every other product on display being for prevention of something, must therefore be designed to stop people having sex.

"Then I shall not buy that for you," she said matter of factly and with a very straight face.

They linked arms and held hands as they stopped to watch the view from the pathway and the people walking by. Small children ran alongside their parents, brothers and sisters, and small babies were clutched tightly by mothers as they walked along. There were a few people who seemed to be sleeping rough near the docks, their blankets and one mattress warming in the sun on a stone wall near where they sat.

The day warmed up and the sun shone in the blue sky as the afternoon progressed, only the faintest of wisps of high cloud showing in the sky.

Reality kicked in sharply as they were watching a small boat heading out to sea. The days were passing with seemingly increasing speed and soon she would be leaving the boat, and him. She spoke first although it had been on his mind too.

"I have thought a lot in the last few hours and I need please to know what you think. I do not wish to be alone for long. You have become very important in my life and I would like that to continue. But only if you have the same feelings for me. Tell me please truthfully what we should do about this."

This was not a time for him to joke. It required a quick response which he gave.

"My feelings are the same, they haven't changed. I want to be with you as much as possible. Maybe we should live together as much as we can?"

"Yes," she said, "that I would like. But where?"

"The simple solution might be to swap living places as we are now doing with our cabins, but between Copenhagen and London. What do you think?" he ventured.

"Every night swap places?" she challenged, jokingly.

"Possibly every month or more to fit around your work, our friends and family, and other things we may wish to do," he suggested.

"That sounds good. Can we work this out in detail before I leave the boat?" she asked him.

"I'll take a look at my busy social calendar and see where I can squeeze you in. I might need though to spend some time consulting my wonderful attractive, sexy, leggy blonde personal assistant on the matter."

"Have you really got one of those?" she questioned, her features showing perhaps a little concern.

"Yes," he replied slowly gazing affectionately into her eyes and taking her hands in his, "if you would like the job."

As they sailed away in the late afternoon the sea glittered in the sunlight and the funfair came to life with some rides and the big dipper working, plus lights and music that followed them over the bay. Three birds dived into the harbour, and behind them was a small beach, backed by little painted houses, where people were swimming. In the far distance ahead of them over the bay were again the high snow-covered peaks of the Andes.

Life was very good, and their sleep was very peaceful.

Day 45

38.0 degrees South, 74.1 degrees West

Total nautical miles travelled by midday — 13,180

This was a day for relaxation. The Pacific had calmed and there was a long, slow following swell, gently rocking the boat in the clear blue sun-filled day. But the breeze was cold, apparently carried by the Humboldt current along the coast and so they sat in sweaters on the balcony and watched the sea looking out for whales that had been reported earlier from the bridge.

There was little to do and so they did exactly that, talking sometimes, holding hands, falling briefly asleep and going to get food. In the afternoon they made gin and tonics and then, totally relaxed, returned to bed to hold each other closely enjoying the quietness and the physicality. One guest speaker on board had promoted the importance of touch in human relationships. They had not needed to be told; it was natural to both of them.

"Think you may find it's gins and tonic, the plural that is."

"Go away, I was on the edge of sleep then."

"OK, but I reckon I'm right. See you!"

He slept, noticing unconsciously her scent, and the smoothness of her hair and skin, the curve of her spine, and the angle of her shoulder blade. And the suppleness and strength of her fingers intertwined with his as her slow breathing mirrored his own.

Late afternoon they went on deck. The sun was now warm, and the breeze had gone. They found seats and enjoyed the sunshine watching passing fishing boats on the blue/green sea, and giant white clouds over the distant mountains beyond the coast. But the whales did not come.

After dinner and a show, they slept ready for an early start when they arrived the following day at their next destination.

Today had been uneventful but still extremely satisfying.

Day 46

33.3 degrees South, 71.3 degrees West

Total nautical miles travelled by midday — 13,473

They docked in San Antonio, Chile and breakfasted before agreeing to see what tours they could pick up at the port terminal. They went through security and looked around the options for visiting Santiago where they thought others might join the two of them to make up minimum numbers for a minibus. That attempt failed and they waited until another option appeared with a minibus and guide going to Valparaiso. They jumped at that rather than having no tour and ended delighted to have done so.

There was a long drive to and from Valparaiso and they looked around the city and walked a little, and then ended up driving into the edge of the poor housing district which ran up every hill as far as the eye could see, perched on wooden or metal legs with the houses backing onto the slope. They were all vividly coloured and many had impossible verandas supported by thin timbers lashed together, creating a patchwork view of the hillsides.

This was a serious earthquake zone and much damage had happened as recently as 2010 and 1985. The lady guide said that they liked earthquakes, but they found that hard to believe even though modern buildings were now constructed to withstand them.

The return was through a fertile wine-producing valley and they stopped to taste some incredibly good local wines served in generous portions in beautiful surroundings overlooking the valley and vineyards. As it happened, they had both enjoyed Chilean wines for many years and these were certainly no exception. They chatted with the guide and driver in bad Spanish and pretty good English and suggested buying them a drink after the tour, so the group was dropped off and they were driven to a local bar where they were joined by a friend of the guide, and drinks were enjoyed although orange juice only for the two locals who would later be driving home.

It was a magical hour, communicating badly from a language perspective but perfectly from the view of human engagement and all enjoyed the brief time exchanging views on the world, life and love. Email addresses were exchanged in haste before the driver departed and the guide drove to the dock where they hugged goodbye and made the gangplank with a comfortable five-minute margin before being late to embark and thus left behind on the quayside.

He told her that he thought the world might be better if people drank a little and learned other languages. He felt good and had very warm feelings towards the Chileans he had met who were genuinely friendly and clearly valued tourists visiting to aid their economy.

As they sailed, the ship turned in an extremely tight area of the dock assisted by two tugs. With horns sounding, the tugboats left with their crew waving and then the two pilot boats also waving whilst on the coastal road by the harbour, cars were stopped and people were waving, whistling, and using car horns as a farewell while a helicopter flew overhead filming maybe for a news item.

Even allowing for the effects of alcohol, this was a very emotional departure that had them feeling a little sad to be leaving such a vibrant and welcoming place.

As if to echo all this, as the sun was setting, and they were enjoying pre-dinner drinks on the balcony, they spotted a puff of white above the water. Grabbing the binoculars, they scanned and found another. It was the plume of spray from a whale surfacing and venting, and it was followed by many others over a distance off the side of the boat. Finally, they saw more than simply the spout and a disturbance in the water as one whale broke the surface with a long grey back and dorsal fin. It was a pod of whales perhaps with their young and seemingly unbothered by the noise the ship must be making as the engines throbbed and the other sounds from the ship penetrated the water.

They hugged and reflected yet again, at their incredible good fortune. They were lucky to see so much where perhaps others didn't even notice.

They again slept well, intertwined like vines.

"Bit obvious that simile?"

"Excuse me, I'm trying to sleep."

"So sorry, but I was awake. See you."

Day 47

29.5 degrees South, 71.2 degrees West

Total nautical miles travelled by midday — 13,701

As they were getting dressed and the vessel was nearly in port, the ship broke. The TV and lights went out and apparently the lifts and a toaster in a restaurant stopped working. The commodore made a reassuring announcement that there was no risk but that the arrival time was going to be later than planned as two tugs were needed to tow the liner to her berth. They were working on putting things right and would keep everyone informed.

Something was amiss and he half expected a marine equivalent of 'is there a doctor on the flight?' except in this situation an engineer or mechanic perhaps would be needed. He reflected on how it might have been had this happened at Cape Horn. The absence of two tugs there would presumably have made the ship very vulnerable.

It was not going to stop them going ashore in Coquimbo as their last stop in Chile, so they had breakfast and left the boat to have fun. They located a minibus trip to the neighbouring resort town of La Serena, and then inland to the Elqui Valley which they had read was a centre of mystical energy, and the production of the local liquor pisco, plus home to many international observatories due to the exceptional clarity of the air. Shooting star sightings were stated in a guide book to be 'every couple of seconds', with UFO sightings also apparently very common.

They toured a local pisco distillery in the green and fertile valley where they drank a couple of cocktails made from this local brandy equivalent. They saw no aliens but wondered how many UFO sightings were linked to over-consumption of local alcohol.

The valley as a whole was fed by a river of snow meltwater and was a major agricultural producer, evidenced by fields of crops along the Ruta de las Estrellas — how he wished it translated as road to the stars, rather than of the stars. Although they had left grey overcast skies on the coast, the valley was sunny and hot with crystal clear blue skies and it was hard to believe that they were actually in the Atacama Desert, the driest desert on earth where a recent drought had lasted many years. Sensibly, the valley had been dammed to create a large expanse of glinting water.

As they drove further, fields of vines appeared inching up the hillsides from the river and ending where sparse scrub and grey cactus plants poked through the rocky barren soil, with the distant backdrop of the peaks of the Andes.

They felt fortunate to witness such spectacular beauty in a landscape they had visited only by chance because that tour was available, and he told her that years back he had heard someone say that everything is exactly as it is meant to be. She liked that philosophy and agreed that it was her experience of life also. They were indeed very lucky people.

In the valley and also opposite where the ship was docked, they saw more of the simple rickety wooden housing on hillsides, supported by wooden poles at the front and all painted in bright colours. They thought that the age of these buildings indicated that they withstood earthquakes well, possibly flexing rather than breaking, and there must be great pride to spend very hard-earned income on the large quantities of paint needed to cover the modest buildings.

They did not observe any stars or celestial bodies on their travels. She observed that it was probably because it was still daylight. He wondered aloud, as the stars were always there and very bright because each was a sun, why a strong telescope couldn't see through the light. Surely with a darkened lens that should work? She knew he was playing but still gave him a look that implied both lunacy on his part and enormous liking on hers. When she eventually came to learn his youthful name of 'Brilliance' she would fully understand the reason for it.

Returning to the boat, hoping it had been repaired, they saw on the enormous bulbous lump just above the water at the front of the ship that a very large seal had climbed onto it and was sunbathing there. The lump was to cut through the water at cruising speed so as to avoid a very large bow wave. It was not designed for seals, but the seal didn't know that.

They sailed early evening and after dinner went onto the aft deck for a talk on the stars and navigation. It was very cold, but the stars were remarkable with the lights turned off, until cloud appeared and blocked the sky, thus prompting them to return to the cabin to warm up and sleep.

He said that it was a pity that the night had not been clear but that instead he would look into her eyes to see galaxies there.

Day 48

24.8 degrees South, 71.2 degrees West

Total nautical miles travelled by midday — 14,013

The boat had rocked gently in the night and they were still off the coast of Chile with only occasional views of the distant last. The sun shone although it was not hot. The sea rolled on long waves and for some time was an almost luminous cloudy green shade, possibly from algae in the water they guessed.

To pass the time, they attended three lectures and walked the decks as well as sitting on the balcony where the rocking had them dozing.

In conversation in a lift, a couple told them they had booked another cruise 'from Japan over the North Pole to Alaska.' The couple left the lift before they could respond but they had obviously been joking or needed a serious course in geography and an explanation of the difficulty of dragging a large ship over the polar ice, perhaps with a very big team of huskies.

It was amazing what people said on board and they exchanged stories. She had heard about 'almost unique' experiences during a talk about tours ashore, and he about someone being 'surrounded on three sides' by ice. He also told her about several very mature ladies chasing men… away. They said that they 'didn't want any of that stuff' which implied that the process of making their babies had not fulfilled them, let alone any further sexual intimacy in their relationships. In every case the husbands were dead. It can hardly have been from exertion in bed, but how unfair that the ladies were on the cruise with the proceeds of savings, while the men were now incapable of travel.

It was strange how time was swallowed doing so little on a cruise. They had not swum or enjoyed the hot tubs as the weather had not yet been warm enough. Nor had they danced other than in the disco. He had told her a little about his cruise work, so she was aware of his dancing abilities although he said he was out of practice. She persuaded him to practice with her and, as tonight was formal dress, they agreed to go to

107

the ballroom after dinner. As they prepared and watched from the balcony, they saw movement in the water and a large number of dolphins passed close to the boat, heading astern, breaking the surface and sometimes leaping above the water with large splashes. She said that they were showing them how to really dance. She kissed him in delight at more magic.

Later in the ballroom they danced to a number of familiar tunes played by the band. They waltzed, quick-stepped and fox-trotted capably and she proved to be a good dancer. Their jive was initially a little rusty until they coincided their movements, but she picked up the samba and rumba effortlessly. Their closeness took over and they wondered why they had not done this days ago. Her dancing was agile and supple, and she moved elegantly to his delight and admiration.

Much later they went onto the darkened rear deck and looked at stars, although the visibility was limited due to the bright moon and some cloud again.

He told her there were stars in her eyes as he took her to bed. And the voice in his head simply whispered to him —

"Sleep well, you must be tired. I'm exhausted by all the dancing. Goodnight."

Day 49

18.2 degrees South, 70.1 degrees West

Total nautical miles travelled by midday — 14,361

They woke to a sunny morning berthed in Arica, Chile, and had a hasty breakfast before heading ashore in search of more adventure.

They located a taxi offering a tour into the desert and were joined by two dancers from the ship who also wished to do the same tour. They were good company and the friendly driver took them to ancient geoglyphs made from rocks placed together on the desert hillsides depicting llamas and people dancing. An early form of graffiti, they surmised.

They also visited a museum with mummies older than in Egypt and out into the Atacama Desert where, in contrast to the fertile river valleys, nothing grew at all. The sand and rock landscape was totally barren with the only movement a dust storm circling and lifting dirt into the sky in wisps resembling mist, and vultures circling on the up-draughts from the cliffs.

As he observed, an interesting place to visit but you wouldn't want to live there. The city of Arica was, however, blessed with constant warmth year-round, of 33 to 35 degrees Celsius leading to its name of City of Eternal Spring but water was scarce and the poverty was plentiful in the rough basic shacks on the outskirts of the town. Even there, people had such nationalistic pride that there were numerous Chilean flags flying. The people they met were again very friendly.

Returning to the boat he realised that he had forgotten to take his hat from the taxi — he hoped that the driver might find it useful.

Speaking later on the boat it was clear that Chile had left its mark and charm on many visitors. After dinner and a show, they slept well with the balcony door propped open for the warm night air and the gentle sound of the sea lulling them to sleep.

Day 50

15.6 degrees South, 75.1 degrees West

Total nautical miles travelled by midday — 14,680

They attended a fascinating lecture about the building of the Panama Canal as it would be the first transit of the canal for both of them. They decided then on another first and went for beer with fish and chips in the onboard pub. She was familiar with this having spent time in London when she was younger.

She told him that she had accompanied her long-term lover there some time after she had completed her degree in psychology and started her career in television. She added a little more information about her lover to what she had previously said. The lover had been a few years older and was making his name as an independent television and film producer which was where they had met. He was a little 'avant garde' and 'arty' which was part of the appeal to her, she now realised, particularly as her middle-class parents — her father working in car sales and her mother a housewife from a small farming background — had intensely disliked her suitor. That was another motivation for her liking him, plus, she said, they had good sex.

That was a prompt for the question of what makes good sex and she was not in the slightest fazed when he asked her outright. Her answer, unhesitatingly, had been that it was about fulfilment, so he asked her if their sex now was fulfilling. In response, she asked what he thought, and then added that if she were to apply her knowledge of psychology to his question, she would infer insecurity. Her smile was infectious. He replied that he was not insecure but he sure as hell didn't want to be second best or to lose her. He smiled with her and then she asked what he thought was good sex.

"Well, fulfilment can be on more than one level," he said, "in terms of satisfaction, pleasure, relaxation and intimacy. You give me all that. But" he paused, "there can be something different too that adds to the fulfilment." She looked anxious and so he added quickly, "I'll tell you about it sometime."

"Can't you tell me now?" she asked coyly.

"Later is better for me," he replied, "but I promise there's nothing to upset you. I just need a drink or two before." He gave her a reassuring smile and held her, looking into her eyes. "You can trust me," he said, "it's just a matter of timing."

She looked back gently. "I choose to trust you with my life," she said. "Tell me when you are ready." She kissed him softly.

The sun was hot, and the cloudless blue sky gave way to a haze towards the shores of Peru ten miles away, a desert landscape of pink and beige mountains falling to the sea in cliffs and long stretches of flat coastal plains.

It was time for the pool, and she asked nothing more about their conversation. He knew now even more how special this lady was. The pool was warm but it was a strange experience being moved around in the water by the motion of the boat, a sort of twitch and pushing or pulling like a bobbing cork as the pool water spilled over within the confines of a retaining wall, side to side and front to back Not at all unpleasant but odd, nonetheless.

The hot tub afterwards was gentler and even warmer, adding to their relaxation. A Caribbean band started playing, creating the sense of an exotic holiday, or if the mood wasn't with you of something very contrived but OK. They had already spoken about it, but the situation eventually highlighted how little they liked people in groups, although they loved many individual people in their lives, and several friends they had made onboard. In concentrations, people seemed to behave less well but they conversely also evidenced some inbuilt need to congregate. It reminded them of films of nesting penguins competing for space and snapping at anyone overstepping some invisible sense of a physical or behavioural boundary.

The cabin beckoned for peaceful relaxation, to shower and change and to doze a little in readiness for dinner. And to watch a solitary whale spout and surface a few times as the boat passed him or her making his or her graceful way to somewhere and doubtless speaking whale-speak to friends miles away in the ocean of "Another of those enormous noisy throbbing surface-swimming monsters that I got a bit of a look at but still couldn't work out. Just like the others it couldn't even be bothered to stop and say 'hello'. No breeding and not worth the time of day I reckon."

They found it amusing to note that the whale appeared to be a 'loner' and not in any group.

"I'm back! Don't wish to interrupt but you do realise that whales have also been around for a very long time with, it seems, little change in their evolution."

"Where did that come from? You've been very quiet for a while."

"I know. Been gathering bits of information. Did you also know that recent research indicates that zebras developed stripes to confuse flies and hence keep them away?"

"So, why didn't horses etc. do the same? And while we're on the subject why is the noise of flies so annoying and why aren't they also annoyed by the sound they make? And why in contrast is the noise of bees so calming?"

"Haven't a clue. I only popped in with a couple of observations for you in case you were getting bored. But I see you're not, so I'm off again. Cheerio."

Day 51

12.3 degrees South, 77.8 degrees West

Total nautical miles travelled by midday — 14,943

They berthed early alongside in Callao, Peru, where they could see very little in the heavy mist. They breakfasted and went ashore where they took a shuttle bus to a shopping mall and then found people from the boat to share a taxi to go into the capital Lima.

They had read that Lima is fog-shrouded for eight months of the year due to the influence of the cold Peru ocean current. The city sprawled, and on the drive there they saw architecture ranging from rough slum dwellings to modern blocks with strong Spanish influences particularly in the old city centre near the Plaza Mayor. There, elegant facades and balconies lined narrow streets and tree-lined squares. Notably the best buildings like everywhere else in the world seemed to be occupied by government departments or dignitaries.

As the sun broke through, the heat increased, and their friendly and helpful driver showed them around on foot as well as in the vehicle. His English was good. From Lima centre they went to the coastal resort of Miraflores where there were surfers and motorised hang-gliders plus what probably were elegant apartment blocks and hotels. Except that the fog had returned, and visibility was very limited. They had lunch in a fish restaurant and drank Peruvian pisco sour. Both Chile and Peru claim this drink as their own. Both versions were equally good.

The taxi took them back to the shuttle bus for the boat and they looked firstly in the large shopping mall where they had been dropped off. It could again have been in any major city in the world as all the stores were the same and there was little if anything obviously local.

Returning to the boat, they relaxed on the cabin balcony, had an early meal in the buffet, and drinks on the balcony as they sailed away passing many boats awaiting their turn to load and unload in the busy port. Then, exhausted, they fell asleep early in a close embrace after again telling each other how extraordinarily lucky they were to be here, and together.

And how they wished it never to end.

Day 52

7.2 degrees South, 80.3 degrees West

Total nautical miles travelled by midday — 15,298

The sea was calm and the sun shining on another day at sea.

"I've decided that I'm going to tell you what I couldn't talk about the other day," he said slowly.

"Your darkest secret?" she asked. "About good sex? Is it really full of juice as you say in English?"

"A little juicy, as we actually say in English," he corrected gently with a big smile, "but not exactly completely full of juice."

He explained that the dark secret was from his days on the cruise liners where his contract was to sing with the band for a certain number of performances each week and additionally to do a small amount of entertaining including karaoke sessions, and standing in for bingo and musical quizzes if someone else on the entertainments team was indisposed. For this, he had a small salary plus board and keep, with free days to go ashore.

He was paid additionally to act as a dance partner for several evenings each week because his agent had negotiated a contract on that basis. He could dance sufficiently well to do this and he was young and in good shape and this came in addition to the main job of singing. He was told that he was attractive and stylish by a number of people and he noticed that this started to become a pattern with some of the more mature, mostly American, lady passengers. The vast majority were widowed but some were travelling alone or with friends, usually also female.

It became most noticeable when having complimented him on his looks, dancing, singing or any combination of those, the mature lady he was partnering then indicated how lonely her life was without a male partner, husband, lover, and how her (inherited) wealth was hers to spend as she pleased and that life was for living after all, wasn't it, and who would blame her for finding pleasure and solace where and when she could, particularly on a romantic cruise in the warm seas with the moon shining over the water and a large stateroom with such a comfortable king size bed so empty? Or words to that effect.

If there was evidence, as there often was, of quantities of expensive Dom Perignon or similar champagne having been consumed by the lady, then she would typically lean forward, brushing his arm with an ample Hermes or similar silk-encased breast and in a suggestive haze of Dior, Chanel or similar perfume whisper in his ear in a very hypnotic manner that she "Yearned to achieve — please excuse me for being so… so direct but we are two grown up persons are we not — orgasm… There! I dared to say it. But you do understand, don't you, the sense of that loss for a very passionate woman? Full satisfaction… forgive me again, with a skilled and sensitive younger man, and that there was nothing wrong with that was there? Or of 'looking after him' for his time or if that was too blatant of giving him a little memento or perhaps a modest sum of money to buy something to remember her by, as she hoped he would, and perhaps if they got on really well that they might do it another time or several times even on this voyage and that wouldn't it be wonderful to visit her for a few weeks holiday in her very modest, but not really all that modest really, you understand don't you, waterfront home near Tampa, Florida, with just one small mooring and motor cruiser plus a couple of jet skis on which he could enjoy himself doing other manly things when they were not passing the time playing in the large dolphin-shaped pool or the hot tub, or even the double hammock? Or had she been too forward? The drink you know… and the heat of the moment? Doesn't sunshine and warmth in the Caribbean affect everyone in this way? You will have noticed that, won't you?"

And that "She did hope that she had not been too presumptuous in suggesting this but why not have another dance? And then she would go to her stateroom numbered 321 or whatever to slip into something more comfortable and so much less restricting and she hoped he liked ladies in stockings and black silk underwear which she always wore and why didn't he discreetly follow her in about fifteen minutes and she would order another bottle of Dom Perignon or similar to be ready for them and that she was almost bursting with the anticipation."

And after the one further dance, the lady would be gone, pink-faced and weaving as he stood stupefied by the experience.

"So, did you go? Is that the dark secret, you naughty boy?" she asked, her grin so wide it was enticing.

He sensed that he could take time over the story as she seemed so relaxed with it so far.

"Oh, I can be a naughty boy, but you need to hear more before you have the complete picture to pass judgement."

He went on to tell her that his and everyone's contracts specifically prohibited any association with guests in their cabins and that after the first few encounters and propositions along those lines, he had worked out how to bring this limitation into conversation at the first intimation that it was about to take a turn in that direction. The first hint from his dance partners was usually a thigh pressed against his for just a little too long during a dance step, often with the sensation of the tell-tale lump of a suspender, or of the thigh pushed a little too much against his groin in a dance as if assessing his potential in the manhood stakes and whether he could rise to any challenge that might be thrown at him.

"You must have enjoyed that," she said still smirking, "spill the peas."

"You're becoming as impatient as those ladies, and the expression is 'spill the beans'. Wait, and I'll tell you the full story," he said.

Sometimes, he went on, it was just that he knew what was about to come and wanted to avoid any embarrassment. So, he would bring the contract terms and the risk to his livelihood into his easy chat early on and soften the impact by talking in the third person about a colleague who had fallen foul of this and lost his job.

It worked. The propositions mostly stopped as did some of the thigh pressing, but by no means all. He realised that his role was viewed partly as social and partly as a target plaything.

"Like a toy for a lady to use," she said.

He paused before laughing at her use of words and the possible ambiguity but then he thought that she probably meant it exactly as it came out and he did not correct her although he could not shake the mental image of him as an object purchased from a sex-shop.

The next stage, he told her, was that he began to feel uncomfortable about having to explain things when in some cases he was making assumptions, possibly because the lady at the time was not a good dancer and the thigh contact was more about her balance on a moving boat than about sexual frustration. The alternative was that it was indeed intended to be an initial sexual approach in a non-verbal way, a sort of preliminary probing as it were. There was no way initially of knowing which.

In either case his conscience was unhappy. These were customers for whom he was paid to give pleasure. They were looking for pleasure and he had some difficulty rationalising the difference between the pleasure from dancing closely to music on the dance floor and moving together in a somewhat more intimate fashion, whether to music or not depending on personal preferences.

"Did you then make love to them? It would be fine if you did. This is ancient history," she said still smiling.

"I'm coming to that," he said, "nearly there."

He outlined his thoughts then. The ladies had a need, they were mature, consenting adults and they were lonely, missing the intimacy of a relationship and doubtless the thrill of sex and of feeling they were attractive to a man, or just still attractive full stop. And they were missing closeness and company. 'Fuck it,' he had thought, 'I'm a man and I used to use sex to find love, although that seems predominantly to be a female thought process. They are paying serious money to be on holiday on this boat and they are prepared to pay to have some romance added. Every other extra on board has a cost. Something is wrong here.'

He had mulled this over for quite a time. It was a challenge. The expression 'horns of a dilemma' kept coming back to him and eventually he renamed it 'his horny dilemma'. There was a solution and it was a good one if he could pull all the parts together. He took it upon himself to take the necessary steps to provide a social service that would have potentially enormous benefits for everyone involved.

Several weeks later and the plan went into operation. He was dancing with a quite attractive lady from Vermont who opened the bidding with her version of the standard script. He explained the problem with his contract terms but then added that he was not averse to being a little flexible in the interpretation although he was sure she would understand the enormous risk to him and the need for this to be reflected in the arrangement, together with the requirement for absolute discretion. Not a word of this must get out to her friends on board, female jealousy being such that a third party could destroy everything, and certainly not in any correspondence or communication to anyone outside the vessel as this could be intercepted, and absolutely not to any member of the crew.

He mentioned also the issue of risk and reward, in that she would understand there must be appropriate inducement for taking the risk. Without him needing to mention specific amounts of money, there was immediately an opening offer on the table as it were. It was a sum well within the range he had mentally targeted and so he moved onto step two of the process.

That evening at eleven p.m. ship's time, precisely as agreed, the passenger lay in bed in the dark, having extinguished the lights and with the stateroom door open with the deadlock activated so that the door was kept slightly ajar. She had, as arranged, placed the cash in an envelope on the floor just inside the room and she knew that the rules of engagement meant that there would no conversation and hence no difficult personal questions on either side. Discretion would that way be assured, as would safety, with protected sex throughout an absolute requirement.

The familiar shape appeared briefly shadowed in the light from the corridor. The intake of her breath was apparent as she heard him undressing and then felt the large mattress dip as he slid beneath the light duvet and inched towards her, his hands finding the softness of her body as he leant towards her and they kissed. It was electric for her. Her body shuddered involuntarily, and a familiar tingle moved through her, quickly reaching deep into the heart of her femininity. It was some time ago that she had last felt this with a man and her anticipation mounted. He reached skilfully for her thigh pulling her towards him and gently eased the hem of her silk nightdress as he stroked her lower back and leg, kissing her gently all the while. She began to make small sounds and he imagined that she might be thinking that the monetary arrangement was very satisfactory particularly when compared to the cost of the onboard beauty salon treatments, which could not possibly ever give so much satisfaction.

Eventually, he eased her nightdress over her head, and they lay together naked as they explored each other's bodies in anticipation of the eventual finality that was so much anticipated. She was aroused, and teased him in all the ways she remembered from days long gone. Finally, she pulled him towards her and climbed over him forcing herself onto him where she used her full New England equestrian skills to ride him to the outer reaches of paradise, ecstasy and oblivion.

Then, she eased off him and pulled him over her for the return ride. As they relaxed, he kissed her and stroked her hair and body until the exhausted lady slept in blissful contentment. He dressed quietly and collected the envelope left on the floor before silently letting himself out of the stateroom to head back to his cabin for a short whiskey and a deep sleep.

"You are indeed a very naughty boy, I think," she said looking at him with a mix of admiration and perhaps a little regret.

"I need to finish the story before you deliver final judgement," he responded with a soft smile.

He continued the story and told her that the next day, or at any other times, it had been agreed that there would be no conversation about the previous night. A discreet smile to him would indicate satisfaction far better than any complex tick-box feedback form could do, and a repeat booking arranged during a dance that evening would certainly prove the worth of the experience as would any small monetary gift slipped discreetly into his palm.

This proved to be a very effective and happy win/win longstanding arrangement and he built up quite a nice little nest egg in his Caribbean bank account, as well as making several property investments with the proceeds.

In fact, he went on now to tell Sofia it was better even than just win/win in that there was another part to the equation, making it win/win/win. He had enlisted a number of crew members to help out, particularly when there were multiple bookings on the same night. Each member of the ship's company was recruited on the basis of being a similar shape and build to him, and each fully understanding the need for total discretion, which was an easy ask given that their jobs were also at risk should the whistle be blown. They would always dress in black to ensure only their silhouette was noticeable as they opened the stateroom door, have no sexual diseases — a few dollars to the ship's doctor ensured that they were tested regularly — would always wear protection, would keep their hair at a similar length, again for the appearance in shadow and for continuity if their hair was stroked or touched, would not indulge in anything kinky, would shower before the meetings and would always wear the same aftershave as him so that the illusion in the dark of having had an encounter with him personally would be complete. And that they would keep physically fit and avoid pornography for one day prior to any booking to ensure that satisfaction would be guaranteed.

There was to be no conversation with the lady which ensured that there was no giveaway from a Filipino, Italian, Scottish, Japanese, Irish or any other accent. They would not discuss any of this arrangement with anyone even with other participants, but they would however give him a summary of the events so that he could ensure quality control in the ongoing delivery of this special service, and this build-up of knowledge over a period of time enabled him to use his team members according to their skills, and to utilise the skills of their members for maximum impact.

The most difficult and delicate part was to ensure that all other ingredients were as uniform as possible. He could not bring himself to ask personal details about their manly endowments nor was he going to check them himself, so again the ship's doctor was enlisted to ensure uniformity in this department. This was essential in the case of repeat bookings as any difference in the size or feel of this critical aspect would blow the cover. The doctor helpfully told him that size was indeed important to a lady and so an optimum range of length and girth was determined and maintained in the vetting process. At an early stage, one Organ Morgan from Neath in South Wales and of the engineering department was eliminated. They had mistakenly thought he was bragging with his nickname or that he was a church goer and so had recruited him as a potential player and asked the doctor to check him. The doctor indicated that if anything he was being modest, and his bragging had been dramatically understated. As to the nickname, the word 'monster' sadly did not rhyme with Morgan. Whilst the crew member was disappointed on one level not to be able to offer a helping hand, or other attribute, in the arrangements, the compensation for him of having obtained independent verification helped enormously in his attraction to some lady crew members.

And finally, he told her, the split of the proceeds was agreed between them all and was the same for everyone, except it was a little more in his favour because it was understood that he generated the trade, was responsible for the overall operation and security, whilst for them they had the pleasure of a natural outlet for their sexual needs plus some beer money. An entirely appropriate 60/40 in his favour seemed to be quite acceptable and it was accepted by all. While it seemed to the others that 60/40 was only a little in his favour in reality it meant 50% more for him than them. He was pleased he had excelled at mathematics.

And above everything else, in the vast majority of cases, he simply did not want to be in any way physically intimate with most of these ladies. He preferred a quiet drink in his cabin reading a book or watching a film, and he could ensure privacy if he arranged that his cabin mate was one of those on duty that night providing the special service for one of the passengers.

His satisfaction level from providing the service was high both emotionally and monetarily.

"Thank you for telling me," she said, "I was only a little worried what you might say about making love to all those ladies but now that the pussy is completely out of the hat, I can feel good about it."

"As do I," he said choosing not to correct her charming description. He did not want to destroy that delightful mental image. "Nor me," ventured his other voice.

"Think you may find it is 'nor I'. Now go away please. This is a very important story."

"OK, I'm off. I know when I'm not welcome."

They relaxed in the sun on the balcony doing very little except watching the sea and looking at each other affectionately. There was no land visible, but they saw a large number of dolphins jumping out of the water in pairs or threes side by side again in perfect synchronicity heading the opposite way to the boat. Later a group of pelicans flying line astern slowly overtook the boat, gliding just above the surface of the sea with just a rare flap of their large outstretched wings to provide a little lift in addition to the wind that kept them aloft. They commented on how much life there must be in and around the oceans for them to witness these events in the enormous scale of all the seas they had travelled through.

And they slept holding each other.

Day 53

0.5 degrees South, 89.4 degrees West

Total nautical miles travelled by midday — 15,705

Morning found them alongside the jetty in the busy fishing port of Manta, Ecuador. Across the jetty were four large boats, one of which was unloading its frozen catch of very big tuna into containers on the backs of lorries. The boat was specialised for the task with a helicopter on deck, plus several small boats, a lookout tower and giant cranes and winches to haul in the nets.

Manta is the centre of Ecuador's fishing industry, they learned, and there were a very large number of boats in port or moored in the harbour. Doubtless, even more would be at sea. Judging by the size of this catch, and the overall number of boats it concerned them to watch. These were mature fish about the length of a man, and they would no longer be able to produce young. It was impossible to estimate how old they were, but it must be many years and it was hard to imagine that this scale of fishing could do anything other than deplete the stocks of fish in this part of the Pacific. This was not the only country fishing them, so the effect would be multiplied worldwide.

They feared that like many other similar situations, action would only be taken when the industry was at risk because there was too little to catch. By then it would perhaps be too late unless the tuna learned rapidly from the flying fish. They doubted that would happen.

They caught a shuttle bus into the city but resisted buying Panama hats made locally although they were beautiful and good value. They already had one each. One vendor was in full Indian clothing. She said that he had a fine body, as indeed he did, but she also confirmed that she did not wish to stay here with him in Ecuador as an Indian wife. She teased him by saying that maybe things would have been different if they had not met up.

Then to a shopping mall where again it could almost have been anywhere in the world except for the food facilities some of which had local names and menus. Everyone they met was again very friendly and some wanted to know that they thought favourably of their country. They were able to reassure them that even on this very brief visit they were impressed by the cleanliness, the relative quietness and the charming people they had met.

They were amused by two things they saw in a department store. One had a medical department and for sale was a dentist's chair complete with all the attachments of lights, sink etc. It looked ready to go with just a drill to be added. You could probably get that at the local builder's merchant. The price they thought was a quite reasonable 3,051 US dollars. It could give greater reality and a new dimension to the idea of playing a version of doctors and nurses they thought, although suitable clothing for that was available at more modest prices. A set of Indian clothing was not.

The second was a simple packet of cotton curtains with a label that read "wash it gently and it will last forever". They weren't sure if European legislation would permit such a statement. Did 'forever' have a specific timeline? If so, the curtains might outlast him at 320 years plus he told her. Perhaps she should buy a pair to have something to remember him by?

And then he recalled two other signs he loved and wished to share. In Spain near Marbella a sign by a walkway reading 'No entry to strange persons'. And from a set of lights purchased in the UK for a birthday celebration with his family 'For indoor and outdoor use only'. He would have bought them just for that, he said, as it so perfectly described him.

They had a quiet night as nothing appealed in the entertainment choices and they did not wish to dance. But, having given the matter considerable thought, they managed to find other things to enjoy before sleeping.

And they slept deeply and contentedly.

Day 54

4.1 degrees North, 79.5 degrees West

Total nautical miles travelled by midday — 16,026

Late last night as they slept, they had crossed the equator into the northern hemisphere. There was no announcement or celebration in contrast with the southbound crossing. No fireworks or partying and so they had not woken to celebrate the event.

They woke to blue skies and slightly choppy seas some distance off the coast of Colombia. Within a short time, patches of the sea had become reddish brown, but they had no idea why. There seemed to be no large rivers nearby to deposit silt and no other obvious reason. They wondered if the Red Sea was a similar colour.

There was a text message for her to contact her business associate about some possible business and so she arranged a meeting late morning. He was happy to relax and happy for her that there appeared to be something developing from her recent business trip in Argentina. He also realised how much time they had been fortunate to have together and how that could be under threat after their return to ordinary life with other demands on time.

When she returned, she told him how a film distribution organisation could be interested in the idea for a series of programmes, and that it was proposed to arrange a business meeting in Florida when she disembarked. Her excitement was obvious, and he told her how happy he was for her. She said that it should not be allowed to damage their new relationship and that she did not think that her involvement in the project would create any difficulties. She would not let it, if he would not. They celebrated with a drink by the pool and then enjoyed a hot tub before locating two of the few sun loungers which they pulled into the shade as the sun was high and very hot. There they lay holding hands while they filled in a few more blanks about their former lives.

They laughed to themselves too, although they agreed that probably they should not laugh about some of the other passengers. One male wore an incredibly small pair of bright swimmers, known in some circles as 'budgie smugglers' and seemed to want people to notice him. Having seen him, it was hard to take their eyes off him as he decidedly did not have a body to match so that the total picture was ghastly and embarrassing.

Later she would recall the description in her own way as 'parrot pants' and would be gently and good-humouredly corrected. His mental image was wonderful.

And the obese were out in numbers carrying heaped plates of food from the buffets. Some could hardly walk; several had walking aids and often they were paired with a partner of similar size. They had difficulty not feeling smug about being in relatively good shape, but it was clear that much of this obesity must be self-induced and causing or likely to cause health problems. Plus, it didn't seem right that they were paying the same fare and eating at least two times as much. One other passenger had said of these people that it was unreasonable that they should take medical care resources at the expense of treatment for people who didn't overeat. This was getting heavy and contentious, so they agreed to not discuss it further. But, he said, it reminded him in a nicer way about children and sweets. A bag of sweets or a chocolate biscuit or candy bar costs the same for children and adults but in relation to body size, children get a much better deal sweet-size compared with body size, with the smallest children getting the best deal by far.

"So," she commented, "in some ways that is fair then because very big people get very bad value from a normal sized portion."

He had to agree the strange logic of this.

That evening they danced again after dinner. He was very pleased that nobody obese was on the dance floor. The sight would not have been good.

And as he was preparing for bed —

"Just had to pop in again — I/we/you just had this thought re large people and mobility. Stair lifts don't actually lift stairs."

"What?"

"And a walking frame doesn't actually walk." "Go. Away."

"OK, goodnight!"

Day 55

9.7 degrees North, 79.4 degrees West

Total nautical miles travelled by midday — 16,323

The alarm woke them early ready for entering the Panama Canal. Panama City was off the starboard side as the sun rose causing the windows of many of the great number of tall buildings to glint with reflections of gold. The city was large and from a distance looked very wealthy.

The first of several canal pilots came aboard, and they travelled some distance until the first set of locks. The skill with which the great ship was brought into the locks was remarkable with only a couple of feet either side between the ship and the lock walls. They were the maximum size that could go through the original locks, a little over one thousand feet long. They were roped to 'mules', in reality trains running alongside not to pull the vessel as they had thought before, but rather to keep the vessel in the centre of the lock avoiding the concrete walls. The ship went through under her own power and it was impressive to observe.

In the central portion they navigated the lake where tropical green vegetation grew to the water's edge and the water itself was a tropical green. The many islands were the tops of hills flooded when the lake was created as part of the canal. A crocodile was reported but not seen by them, but the air was filled with the cries of exotic birds. Finally, they went through the last locks back down to sea level in the Caribbean, a reversal of the morning's process.

According to two people on board who had reliable credentials the cost of the ship using the canal was in the hundreds of thousands of US dollars, all paid up front before the journey could commence. With fifty ships a day transiting the canal the daily income was probably a few million US dollars, meaning that the government of Panama which owned the canal had a nice little earner, even allowing for wages, repairs and improvements etc.

They passed the time talking and the subject of dictatorships came up having just seen a continent renowned for them. He said that he thought he might be good at that — surely there was a role for a benevolent dictator somewhere? He had never been able to work effectively in committees as so much time was wasted arguing minor points and they achieved so little. He asked her how he might apply for the job, was there a specialist newspaper carrying job advertisements aligned with such characters? How would he word a CV? Or might the local employment exchange, or whatever it was now called, be helpful?

She gave him a sideways look and said that she felt sure that she could help him if there was a role for her and that she might be able to enlarge her shoe collection whilst doing good. Plus, live in a nice home with frequent banquets. She thought there was bound to be an agent for this type of work, and it would be easy to track down the name and an introduction by calling a few existing holders of this type of job.

"I'll do it when I get back," she said, "they're bound to have seen my children's TV series when they were young, and their nostalgia will ensure that they help us."

It was a lovely thought and it almost had a ring of truth as he knew her series had been dubbed into a number of languages. But she said not in South America and so he suggested they keep this idea on the back burner for at least the time being.

The moon rose immediately the sun had set. A giant cheddar cheese coming out of the ocean and brightening as it rose, creating a pathway of shimmering gold across the sea. It had been an early start, so they dined lightly on the aft deck and danced to the music of a good rock band who played music they liked. Then they headed to the cabin where she took the initiative and made love to him skilfully, beautifully and gently. She explained that she was aware how limited their time together on the cruise was and that she wanted him to remember her when they were not together.

He had not needed reminding. It was frequently in his thoughts.

Day 56

13.9 degrees North, 79.4 degrees West

Total nautical miles travelled by midday — 16,605

The Caribbean morning was warm and welcoming with an azure sea, white wave tops and small clouds. They agreed that it was a day to do little except use the pool and the hot tubs and sit around. They debated the difference between being lazy and relaxation and agreed that the debate only came about because of a Protestant work ethic or its other cultural equivalents. Can't be bothered to do anything probably equated to siesta around the Mediterranean and chilling in the Caribbean. Nothing wrong with any of them, they concluded, and hence had clear consciences about their choice over their use of time.

"It's worrying that you're worrying about this."

"I'm not worrying, just checking it's OK to give myself permission."

"Just proved my point, got to go, time to slob out. Bye."

They enjoyed their relaxed day and there was little else that appealed so that simply sitting in the sun, swimming in the pool, or enjoying the warmth of the hot tub was quite acceptable. They dressed for the formal dinner and enjoyed a cocktail at the outside bar by the rear pool. And after dinner just crashed out again in each other's arms expressing gratitude again in what had almost become a ritual, to the gods that had brought them together.

That night they had no anxieties.

Day 57

18.2 degrees North, 77.5 degrees West

Total nautical miles travelled by midday — 16,910

As dawn broke the ship entered the navigation channel for Montego Bay, Jamaica and berthed a little afterwards as they dressed.

He was looking for news on the TV and channel hopping when he caught a documentary about fish and coral reefs. He had dived many years before and she apparently had also done that. The film showed a stonefish which he had only once seen underwater. It was the most venomous fish and to be avoided if you could see it, which wasn't at all easy given its amazing resemblance to a coral rock. He had been gently floating in one spot with snorkel and goggles and hadn't noticed it for fifteen minutes because of its very effective camouflage. The documentary also showed film of a brightly coloured scorpion fish and the commentary said that each of these contained enough venom to kill two hundred mice.

He visualised this and gave her a narrative description of the tiny whiskered animals wearing miniature scuba tanks and masks swimming down to attack the scorpion fish. Up to two hundred would die in the attempt and any excess would survive as might the fish if the attack were unsuccessful. How had anyone come up with such a bizarre statistic? How did the maths work and why would the fish bother to have a defence against such an improbable attack? he asked rhetorically. Surely the mice would avoid the cost of buying underwater equipment and learning to dive when they had easier pickings on land, for example cheese. And how did they know about the existence of the fish. And he thought mice probably did not like water anyway. He would come back to this thought train again.

"You have a very imaginative mind," she said. A millisecond later his subconscious repeated the same words.

"Thank you," he replied aloud to her and subconsciously to himself, "it has served me well over the years."

"What's the point of a rhetorical question?" threw in his subconscious/alter-ego/or whatever.

"You can ignore that, by the way, no need for an answer… Got to fly."

They boarded the shuttle bus to the terminal and then walked to a beach they had read about. It turned out to be accessible for eighty US dollars each via the hotel that owned it, a strange ploy when Hard Rock Cafe next door had a free beach and pool. One hundred and sixty dollars would, they calculated, buy quite a quantity of local Red Stripe beer. After enjoying a few of the beers in the sun with theoretical change from their 160 bucks they caught a free shuttle bus back to the port area.

Wishing to show her the town, they boarded a minibus that took them around and showed them the sights as well as telling them a lot about education, home ownership etc. on the island. As it was a Sunday most shops were closed so they returned again to the port terminal.

They had spotted a restaurant and bar sign nearby and decided to walk to it. It was open and they went in. He wanted to have jerk chicken which he had enjoyed many times on earlier visits to Jamaica and she wished to try it. They ordered it plus bottles of Red Stripe and talked with the friendly waitress.

And then he noticed a sign on the wall 'Brigadoon'. He thought maybe it was the name of a boat as there were many signs and pictures in the cosy little bar. In the middle of the table was the same name and so he asked the waitress if it was the name of the bar. He outlined the story of the musical for her and Sofia, of an American tourist stumbling across a Scottish village that appears only for one day every hundred years. The tourist, he thought played by Gene Kelly, falls in love with a village girl and has to decide whether or not to go back with her, leaving his current life behind. True love prevails and he chooses to be with her. It was one of his favourite childhood musicals with the wonderful song 'Almost Like Being in Love', and he held it and similar Hollywood films responsible for his incurable romantic core.

The waitress pointed to a man sitting at the bar who was the owner and she went to speak with him. The man came over and told his story of how he had worked in London where he originally saw the film which he loved. He also saw it elsewhere five times in total while working, including in Canada, and finally on TV in Jamaica when he returned to live there permanently and buy a property. It happened that driving to work he saw a 'For Sale' sign on an overgrown entrance gateway with a dilapidated house in gardens which had run wild. He knew immediately that he wanted to own the house. He was in competition and it was a close-run thing if he would get it. The name on the broken sign at the end of the driveway was incomplete and it was only when he met the vendor, a Scottish lady, that he learned the property was called 'Brigadoon'. Perhaps it was meant in some way? And his grandfather had been Scottish too. His restaurant and bar were named after the house.

If they could have chosen a more romantic place to eat and hear the tale it would have been hard to beat this. It was by pure chance that they had stumbled on it.

He told her how he had read years ago about coincidences and how when they appeared with increasing frequency it bore witness to tuning in on or becoming more focussed on life in some way. It had been his experience that this was true, and it seemed to be happening again now. His life was very good.

As was their quiet and romantic evening watching the sea and stars before bed.

Day 58

17.4 degrees North, 82.9 degrees

Total nautical miles travelled by midday — 17,197

There was an early announcement from the commodore via the loudspeaker in the cabin about precautionary measures on board due to a number of people having gastrointestinal problems. As more than two percent of the guests onboard were affected, the ship understandably had to take measures to limit this and a notice was being sent to cabins.

In conversation later with other guests, after a breakfast handed out by blue-gloved staff and with cling film protecting food from guests breathing onto it, the risk was apparently also that the ship might not be allowed to dock in Florida unless the problem was sorted before arrival.

This 'play ship' was becoming a plague ship they joked but it was an anticipated risk with so many people in close proximity and serious measures were sensibly being taken. One suggestion was to avoid physical contact, and shaking hands was mentioned as something to avoid. She light-heartedly asked if they would still be able to kiss. He said it was fine, but they would have to limit it, and that they would definitely not be allowed to kiss anyone else.

It made them recall a conversation they had overheard a few days before when two older ladies were discussing strategies for holding parties in their staterooms. The guess was that they were in suites as they were advising each other on who to invite and why not to invite certain other people because they hadn't reciprocated the purchase of coffee, hadn't invited them back after an event, or hadn't said 'thank you' for something or other. Completely oblivious to the irony of not saying 'thank you' at the time, one counselled the other on how to write a belated 'thank you' for something she had attended — "I am so sorry but life on board has been so frantic, darling, that I haven't been able to thank you until now..." or similar.

The debate included whether or not to give presents or to offer champagne and, if so, to purchase on board or by the case in a supermarket in Florida remembering that it would need to be carried to the boat... they would have to consult their husbands who clearly were elsewhere doing something far more interesting.

The conversation took quite some time and it was amusing to hear. They were truly glad that they did not inhabit this world. The health issue on board might also limit the socialising now it had been announced and require even further deliberation. They surmised that ideas by any guests of 'more intimate' types of party involving close contact must now be dead in the water as it were.

At noon the ship's siren sounded and the commodore gave an update, repeating the need for personal hygiene but also updating as usual on the weather and other details — the weed floating by was from the Sargasso Sea and the depth of water was in excess of 5,000 metres. It was again a long way down and they chose not to think too much about it or what might be beneath them. Nothing was evident on the surface until early evening when three dolphins cleared the water in succession, silhouetted against the fiery orange sun dropping into the waves at the bow of the ship.

They enjoyed the hot tub and later cocktails before dinner followed by dancing as another day rolled by.

Day 59

17.2 degrees North, 88.7 degrees West

Total nautical miles travelled by midday — 17,496

The arrival in Belize City, Belize, was early and they went ashore by a tender provided by the port, a fifteen-minute journey over crystal blue water, landing on a jetty where people were assembled for tours, and shops and restaurants welcomed them.

The town was colourful but poor like other Caribbean towns. And the sun shone intensely under a cobalt sky onto the brightly painted but sometimes dilapidated buildings.

They were delighted to see on the front window of a local bus the legend 'Protected by God'. Was no higher power protecting the others? How worthless by comparison did it make the earthly insurance cover advertised by windscreen stickers from terrestrial financial companies look?

The people again were outgoing and helpful, and they asked a girl selling tours about being able to see manatees. There was insufficient time sadly to go in search, but she turned out to be a qualified diver whose father was a local lobster fisherman. Helping him one day she had encountered two manatees sleeping, and she had also dived nearby with whale sharks. They shared diving tales and learned interesting facts including that jaguars apparently did not swim to cross rivers but rather dived under the water to make the crossing. She sounded sincere, although they doubted that she had witnessed it first-hand.

They drank local beers at a bar by the landing jetty for the tender and then returned to the ship. The map on the TV in the cabin showed their position as Tierra del Fuego, a repeating fault that made people wonder jokingly how accurate the main navigation systems were. It had prompted a conversation earlier in the day about not seeing penguins in Belize and why they weren't there. Obviously, nobody had told them about the charms of the Caribbean where they would not need to stand closely packed with others, nestling their solitary egg on their feet with their feathery fronts folded over the egg to keep it warm in the extreme frozen winds of the Antarctic.

There was plentiful land in the warmer islands of the Caribbean and evidently numerous plots for sale where an enterprising and forward-looking penguin could build a small home with water access for a quite modest sum. Surely it would be possible to arrange some advertising and inspection flights and maybe train a few to be real estate agents to kick start the process? Seals can be trained for merely a few scraps of fish after all. They doubted that corruption would become an issue as he knew well it often had in the world of Caribbean and other property transactions. Penguins would be unlikely to take backhanders from property developers if only because they have not yet evolved hands.

"Another flight of fancy from your deranged mind."

"Except penguins can't fly."

"Still a deranged mind."

"Yes. But is it just mine, or are you partly to blame too?"

"Not me, guv. I wasn't there, honest. Got to go, bye."

After the ship sailed, they weaved their way through the illuminated buoys of the navigation channel making tight turns until a white pilot boat emerged from the darkness to take the pilot home and they sailed on.

A substantial segment of the moon shone white on and off between gaps in the clouds. He posed the question as to why a grey lump of rock hanging in the blackness of space could reflect light from the sun to the earth and moreover how the reflected light could be white. He had never done an experiment, but it seemed to him that if you held a piece of coal in a completely dark room and shone a small beam of torchlight onto it that it would still look black. He had no idea if it would even actually reflect light.

She humoured him and suggested that it would be fun sometime to try it and then, exhausted from walking around in the heat, they fell asleep in each other's strong gravitational pull. Along the way to their dreaming the voice interrupted briefly:

"No comment, except to remind you about the need to get a life. Sleep well."

Day 60

18.4 degrees North, 87.4 degrees West

Total nautical miles travelled by midday — 17,580

Overnight they had travelled a relatively short distance along Mexico's Yucatan Peninsula and were alongside now in Costa Maya, Mexico. Two other cruise liners were berthed at the terminal built and owned by an American cruise company and resembling a film set. It was well enough done, with a Mayan temple, bright colours and numerous shops, excursion businesses, and captive dolphins to swim with for those not concerned about wild animals in captivity.

The dolphin pool was small, and it was tragic to observe creatures seen swimming so freely in the expansive oceans sentenced to a life of imprisonment, confined to a very small area. Having also witnessed the history of slavery in so many recent places the parallel was obvious. A large corporation owned the dolphins purely to add to corporate profits and ostensibly to enhance the experience of fare paying travellers. Something was very wrong with that and it upset them both.

Perhaps equally sad was that for the vast majority of passengers their experience of Mexico was based on staying in the sterile artificial surroundings of this area. These visitors saw nothing of the real country and the people.

They walked outside the port area and saw plots carved out for sale from the surrounding jungle each displaying real estate boards. Numerous yellow cabs waited in the hope of passengers, but none appeared to be doing any business because most tourists remained in the comfort, to them, of the unreal bit.

Large lizards sat sunning themselves on the concrete boxes made to await electrical connection to any houses that might happen to be built sometime. There were very few houses actually built. They found a hotel, but it had no coffee shop and no internet connection. That was a first for any hotel in both of their travel experiences. Was this another indication of the false economy carefully contained within the corporate port area to the exclusion of the local community?

They talked as they walked around in the heat. She told him of an experience during her early TV career in Denmark when she first appeared with her creation Owlee, a glove puppet resembling a cute owl with large eyes and stubby wings. She was the story teller in a programme broadcast late afternoon for young children returning from school. The logic was that this was timed to occupy children while mother prepared the evening meal before father returned home to relax after work. The show was broadcast live every night and lasted for twenty minutes initially but was later extended to half an hour when the viewing figures shot up dramatically a few weeks after the first broadcast.

She had pitched the show very accurately for the young target audience. The combination of fluffy appealing creature and her interaction with the puppet worked well and she had the right look for the television of the time being young, slim and she hoped relatively attractive. She had a good voice and an easy manner telling stories ranging from fairy tales to descriptions about everyday life that she wrote herself and which were enjoyed by the young audience.

Unexpectedly, however, the show became a bit of a cult because not only did the children adore her, but she caught the eye of a very large number of fathers. The word spread and she was noticed by and written about in certain periodicals. The female press made much of her wholesomeness while those magazines pitched at male readership made much of her imagined charms. Her reticence and hence refusal to pose in other than wholesome ways actually made her even more appealing. Less is more meets girl next door, she thought, and played this well. Wives did not necessarily notice the effect she was having on their husbands, only that fathers were sitting spellbound, quietly watching TV, huddled with the children and so not getting in the way. The males even started to come home earlier rather than stopping on the way at a local bar as they used to do.

Her popularity increased and she was in time able to negotiate a longer contract for more money but not before being involved in an event she would prefer to have avoided. At the same time, she began regularly to appear in magazines and was frequently photographed and reported upon as a celebrity. It appeared that everybody loved her. Some told her, some sent gifts, but there were other types.

When she had first run the idea for the show past the executives of the TV company, they had thought the concept had possibilities and had been happy to offer a three-month trial period subject only to her agreement to using an old contact of one of the executives as the puppeteer. As the executive had told her in the meeting, she was new to performing and he wanted a safe pair of hands with someone who had been around in the entertainment business for a number of years. Although the older performer would not be visible on camera, he would ensure from his wealth of experience that nothing would go off the rails in the live TV broadcasts.

She had agreed because she thought that she would learn from the puppeteer and he had been quite charming when they were introduced and when she had introduced her puppet character to him. He thought Owlee had enormous potential for which he was sure he could provide great character and personality 'by the skilful and creative use of his hand' as she remembered him expressing it. He was much older with a solid background in theatre and some television and he promised her that they would do great things together.

Everything went well in rehearsals with the puppeteer below a table with the one hand operating the puppet through a hole cut in the table top. She sat behind the table which had a large cloth all around the front to ensure that the puppeteer was not visible to the children. In that simple way the illusion of Owlee as a real creature could be created and maintained. Her role was to interact with the puppet through conversation, and by stroking, patting or prodding him as required during the course of the programme. As the series developed the table became something where she and Owlee could prepare food, play games, or make things which the audience could then do at home. Sometimes Owlee would just sit and listen to her stories, and sometimes he would walk a little on his small puppet feet. The hole was large enough for this and by carefully placing her arm in front of him he could appear to hop and sit on her hand or forearm.

They went live and soon established a following. Owlee was loved, and she was popular. The puppeteer was delightful and managed to give the promised true sense of character to his puppet. All was well for the initial few weeks until the popularity of the show for some reason got the better of the puppet operator. It later transpired that he had a bit of a drink problem possibly known to his TV executive friend but who certainly had not mentioned it to her. There was however another problem that the executive possibly had no knowledge of.

One night she noticed a smell of drink on the puppeteer's breath as they prepared to go live but that was not unusual as she knew that many people on live TV often had a small drink to bolster their confidence, and she also had done that on the first few nerve-racking shows. He settled beneath the table as usual and the hand with Owlee appeared on cue as the show started. She thought his position beneath the table was a little nearer to her than on previous shows, but she continued as usual. His free hand presumably usually supported him as he balanced in some way beneath the table. She had never checked how he did that and never had any need to check it as her involvement was simply with Owlee, through the gloved puppet hand above the table.

During the show, she felt a hand brush her knee briefly and thought he might just be adjusting his position, perhaps a cramp being in a strange position for so long, or perhaps one of his joints was just getting a little uncomfortable. He was after all a little older than her. Nothing showed on her face and she continued unconcerned until the hand touched her knee, and remained there. She was in the middle of a long story; the camera was on her and her professionalism demanded that she revealed nothing. Everything had to look completely normal. Quietly and discreetly she lowered her free hand beneath the table and removed his hand from her knee.

The show ended with nothing further happening and he apologised to her afterwards. Her response was measured when she told him what she would do if it were ever repeated. He appeared to understand and left the studio quietly. She mentioned it as lightly as she could to the relevant executive not wishing to escalate anything. The popularity of the show was increasing, and indications were already being made that there might be the possibility of a longer contract. She would therefore not make any waves.

The puppeteer seemed to avoid eye contact with her for a few more shows until he appeared a little later than usual one afternoon and with a distinctly stronger smell of alcohol, together with indications that keeping his balance was slightly more difficult. They had rehearsed a few days earlier and they readied themselves to go live. It was initially an animated performance with Owlee playing his part well as she talked with him and read a story until the point when his role was to become tired and ready for a little sleep. Owlee lay across her arm. As she read a bedtime story to him, she felt a hand brush her leg. She realised that the puppeteer was probably suffering from some stiffness beneath the table, but she knew exactly where it was located when his hand slipped beneath her dress and onto her thigh. He did not move it away but gave her flesh a small squeeze.

On the TV screens of a great number of Danish families the delightful story continued as Owlee slept. As she continued quietly reading to the sweet puppet, she lowered a hand beneath the table, gripped the hand on her thigh and pulled the fingers sharply backwards until they made a very nasty cracking sound, inaudible to the microphone boom. She held this position for a few seconds then released the hand which was immediately removed from her thigh. To the audience, Owlee appeared to wake and leap into the air momentarily and then contract into a cute little ball on the table next to her arm. With both hands she gently prised open the fluffy cute ball and she placed Owlee gently back onto her arm. There he perched imperceptibly twitching as she affectionately stroked him and addressed the camera saying that poor Owlee had obviously just had a very nasty owl dream.

Owlee was less animated for the remaining twelve minutes of the show. She knew exactly how long because she checked on the studio clock at the time of the event. Eventually, after what she thought probably beneath the table felt much longer than twelve minutes, she finished the story and ended the show saying a goodnight to the children from her and from Owlee. She was very relaxed and extremely pleased with her reaction. To his credit, the puppeteer had made no sound other than the cracking of his finger joints.

The show finished. She got up from the table and watched as the puppeteer emerged looking very grey and holding his damaged hand. As it turned out nothing was broken but he was in extreme pain and suddenly very sober. He looked at her in an odd way that she could not read, and he left the studio. They worked together until the end of the trial period when he left the show saying that he wished to pursue other interests and a young lady puppet operator was recruited and trained for the extended series. Nothing was said by anyone about the event and nothing was observed by the viewing audience. For reasons she could not explain she also did not tell her lover working in TV.

Sofia finished her story as they re-entered the port area. Marc hugged her and told her that he admired her for what she had done. Kissing her, he teased her by saying that he hoped she would never need to remove his hand from her thigh.

Returning to the boat they sat in the sun talking with fellow passengers and spent some time in the hot tub before supper, a drink and bed.

Another day together had gone.

Day 61

23.1 degrees North, 83.5 degrees West

Total nautical miles travelled by midday — 17,937

They were at sea a few miles north of the coast of Cuba and the sun shone. The day cooled however as they approached Florida.

Looking him in the eye, she asked about any previous significant relationships other than his marriages which he had told her about early on, as she had told him about her long-term partner. She asked particularly about his experience of internet dating.

He told her that there had been a lady on one of the cruise liners that he had thought of at the time as important. Her name was Patsy and she was the onboard harpist. Sadly, it had not worked out as it was not totally right for some reason, but they had enjoyed time together for many months. He remembered her well because they used to play a game. She would run her fingers over his back as if she were playing the harp and he would attempt to guess the tune. Because he loved his back being touched so much and understood the mechanics of harp playing so little, he was always slow and frequently unable to get the answer right. In return he would play piano on her back, but she was usually quick to recognise the music which created an imbalance and defeated the object for him of shared pleasure.

And there had also been one time when his entrepreneurial spirit had overlapped dating. This was after he had returned to life ashore.

Internet dating had appeared around that time. It didn't so much burst on the scene as dribble in, but word got out and friends had recommended it to him, in some cases recounting adventurous encounters. For both sexes it represented an easy way to find a potential partner, whether for life or perhaps for a somewhat briefer meeting of minds... and bodies, or in some cases just bodies. The objective of exchanging wedding vows was replaced, it seemed, by the objective of exchanging bodily contact. He had lived through the 'swinging sixties' but somehow seemed then to have missed much of the action. This for many people was their chance to catch up and get even.

He met a few ladies and became good friends with some. A couple of times they came close to pooling business knowledge to create a small business. The most notable was with the finance director of a large company. She was a fully qualified accountant by profession well versed in double entry, and he had studied accountancy in college.

"Is that 'double entry' reference a bit obscure?"

"It's a method of book-keeping."

"And I thought it was a subtle double-entendre."

"Really?"

Shopping for chemist's sundries together, they discovered the very limited range of sexual aids for the more mature. The selection of lubricants was frankly quite boring, and they had many conversations about the hole in the market. Surely it must be possible to create something more interesting, perhaps pitched at the more 'travelled' person.

"Do you realise the Freudian references in that paragraph?"

"Be quiet — my creative juices are flowing."

"All right. Leave you to it. I'm off."

It seemed to them that they should focus on all the senses, or at least as many as could be incorporated in a new product. She had worked with a Taiwanese lady who remained a good friend and she recalled that the lady's brother ran a business manufacturing and exporting industrial oils and lubrication. Perhaps it would not be difficult to modify the principles of anti-friction from earth movers to something that could also move the earth in the right hands, or whatever.

After many months of development and consultation they had a range of test samples that they were happy with. They needed to know how comfortable the world at large was with the resultant products — comfort and satisfaction needed to be high. Would people prefer for example the physical sensory nature of 'Bahamian beach' with the appearance of fine white sand (but definitely not the texture) and the essence of coconut combined with the exotic flavour of mango, or might they prefer 'Essex girl' with added moisture and a smell and flavour associated with a cheaper but popular perfume as used by the younger

145

generation? Also perfect for some role play along the lines of *My Fair Lady*.

They also followed a recommendation from the Taiwanese producer who had apparently spoken at length with his chief chemist who was young and male but also had the advantage of not having travelled either to the Bahamas or to Southend. 'Sweet and Sour no. 69' was their suggestion, apparently based on an item on the menu in a favourite restaurant of theirs.

They approached friends for the initial test-marketing, armed with a total of six products based on diverse geographic names and constituents, in each case designed to unlock deeply pleasant personal memories. Some senses like smell and taste can take people back to very positive memories of earlier times — the scent of a tropical flower, the flavour of food or drink, or the sound of wind in the trees, for example. Some of these could be added to the product to transport people back to times of great pleasure by triggering neurotransmitters in their brains so that the previous delightful experiences would become real and could be relived in the subconscious. They would enter their very own pleasure domes and achieve heightened pleasure in their lovemaking.

Product sales would break records and they would become very rich penetrating the market of penetration.

They had not, however, overcome the challenge of adding sound to the gel and it seemed unlikely that they could quickly do this even with the technology of nano-particles. That aspect could wait a short while and would be a stunning product enhancement after the undoubted, successful launch onto the market.

The plan was that testers would fill in a satisfaction survey during and immediately following use, and they anticipated that some might be asked to attend a focus group to provide feedback prior to the final product refinement.

The market was calculated to be large, lucrative and international. They employed design and brand consultants at considerable cost and over a period of weeks arrived at a product name and identity:

'LUBRIC*NT'

The name was presented in a skilfully designed new typeface and with subtle selected colourings for each of the six individual products reflecting the character of each. The asterisk was a silver star radiating outwards across the packaging with the top right starburst extended towards the top right corner of the packaging. The brand consultant in charge of the product development explained that this was to represent ultimate satisfaction — the explosion of orgasm. He explained that his ultimate satisfaction came from the creative process. In their opinion they too would have achieved spontaneous orgasm if someone had paid them the amount of his fee for coming up with this.

But it was essential, and therefore money well invested. They approached several advertising agencies for indicative quotes and strategies, which they would consider while they awaited the feedback from the test-marketing. Copyright and patents would also need to be dealt with.

All was going swimmingly until a contact from the Advertising Standards Authority invited them to 'pop by for a quiet informal chat'. They both went to meet with them. It appeared that the Authority were 'less than comfortable' about the asterisk in the product name. Someone had alerted them they said. Of course, they could not disclose who as this was just a 'gentle conversation designed to reach understanding'. It did not take great powers of deduction to realise that it could only have been a member of staff from one of the firms they had employed. Doubtless, someone other than from management as they would have no reason to do so, and clearly someone motivated by their view of the public good… and perhaps a killjoy with a problem of premature ejaculation or frigidity.

His lady partner, both in business and in bed, asked them to outline their concerns about the supposedly offending starburst. The reply was given somewhat uncomfortably by the older gentleman addressing them. He was a mature male and very old school. A gentleman who it was clear would prefer not to answer so specifically to an attractive, confident younger lady. She doubted he had ever used the word he was having difficulty uttering except at public school to an offending younger boy. Certainly, never to a lady.

He coughed and moved uncomfortably in his seat as she asked him again to explain the problem. Surprisingly for such an apparently confident alpha male, his cheeks turned pink and he looked decidedly unhappy as he squirmed visibly.

Sensing the discomfort of the senior gentleman who was no doubt his boss, and wishing to help him a younger colleague chirped up.

'Cunt,' he said firmly and in obvious frustration.

'I'm sorry?' was her slow and measured response as she looked him squarely in the eyes. 'Did you just say what I thought you said?' She was enjoying this greatly.

More elderly discomfort and now mild embarrassment from the younger colleague slowly gave way to agreement that this was indeed the concern about the promotion of the product. It did not matter that it was down to the interpretation of the starburst even though that interpretation was entirely in the mind of the reader. The point was that 'Damn near everyone will read it like that, and we cannot offend the young, the old, the impressionable or anyone likely to be offended.'

They should have added QED as every possibility appeared to have been covered.

She asked how FCUK had ever been allowed as a tee-shirt logo but could only elicit a response that this had been 'different'. A rethink was needed.

Frustrating as this was, it was not the final nail in the coffin. That came from the feedback. They had proposed to arrange over a period of time face to face interviews with the friends who had tested it. But the feedback actually came looking for them, and very rapidly.

The product was a joy and did everything it said on the label but with one downside. In several cases in the throes of passionate lovemaking, the sensory stimulation of the wonderful memories had worked perfectly, transporting people back to happy times on holiday or in romantic settings on a beach, in the woods, in the shower, in a meadow of spring flowers etc. etc. It was amazing, they were told by everyone. That was good to hear.

It was a wonderful experience and at first sight nothing sounded wrong. But calling the partner you are making love to by the wrong name is never good. When both partners do it simultaneously while joined so closely it is decidedly not good at all. In ordinary circumstances it can spell emotional death to relationships. In these cases, it had destroyed some relationships and done damage to others. A few remained unscathed and were even able to laugh it off. But they were the significant minority.

Most of the friends said that they could not face using the product again because the embarrassment was too great. Unspoken names of lost loves had surfaced which were not known at all by their partner because the old relationship had been such a closely guarded and very private secret. Particularly when the name was that of a member of the same sex.

The trip down memory lane for the testers had been so real that they felt they were actually there with Roberto, Conchita (or both) in a quiet corner, sheltered beneath the palms on Turtle Beach, Tortola or wherever. The names of the partner they had been with at that time and place just spilled out in the intense passion of the moment. It was an inevitability.

Would they buy the product? Not unless they could find another partner with the same name as the one that had surfaced and, god willing, they would attempt to do that to experience that 'high' again.

The testers were, of course, also now unexpectedly single, back on the market and therefore free to embark on that search. Some even decided to try to track down the long-lost partner.

It was not the reason his relationship with the very personal business partner had ended but the loss of a creative dream and of some hard cash probably contributed, he explained.

"That is a truly lovely but sad story for you," she said pulling him to her. "Do you perhaps have any samples remaining that we could try?"

"I would be happy to do that," he said, "except for three things — we destroyed all of it because nobody wanted it, even for free; secondly, I don't want you to call me the wrong name or vice versa, and thirdly, and certainly most importantly, we don't need it. I visit paradise when I make love with you — anything else would be a disappointment."

She kissed him hard. "It's our last day for some time, let's have cocktails in the Commodore Club to watch the sunset, and order room service with champagne then you can make slow love to me and call me any name you like."

"Done," he responded, and they did exactly what she had proposed.

Day 62

26.5 degrees North, 80.7 degrees West

Total nautical miles travelled by midday — 18,232

Although they had mentally prepared for it, the day had arrived too quickly and they were soon ashore in Fort Lauderdale, Florida, queuing for Immigration. She was going with her business associate to a series of meetings in and around Miami and a car was waiting. They held each other, kissed and reaffirmed their love, promising to keep in contact as he crossed the Atlantic and as she finished in Florida and flew home to Copenhagen. They had agreed that they would arrange dates for their future meetings and visits to each other's homes and for holidays and other trips over the forthcoming year or so. The plan was that he would visit her firstly in her flat in Copenhagen as he had never been there. Introductions to friends and family could also be made.

As they kissed goodbye with tears, he could not know that it would not work out that way.

They waved and blew kisses as they went their separate ways and he boarded a shuttle bus to visit a shopping mall for a few items he needed. He found leather shoelaces and a belt, and he ate lunch. But it was lonely, and he already missed her a lot.

It was an uneventful day and so he returned late afternoon ready for the ship's departure. He was in time for the emergency drill.

His evening was about passing time. A drink, dinner with the friends on the ship that she had said goodbye to yesterday, a walk on the deck as they sailed the Florida coast towards Port Canaveral, and finally to bed.

He had known that it would feel empty and he emailed to say that he missed her. She responded similarly. Her hotel bed felt empty too, she said. It was going to feel strange for some time, not least when he half woke in the night and felt for her touch, then briefly panicked at her absence until reality kicked in.

"You'll soon get over it."

"Fat lot you know about it."

"OK, but you forget, I've been around a long time. Try to get more sleep."

Day 63

28.2 degrees North, 80.3 degrees West

Total nautical miles travelled by midday — 18,375

Another short overnight run brought him early morning to Port Canaveral again. He had been alone the last time, but on this occasion, he felt it.

Taking a shuttle bus, he went to Cocoa Beach and walked to the river in the hope of seeing manatees. He was told by a local lady that they were around but they didn't show up for him and so he changed direction and headed to the beach. There was a festival of surfing and skateboarding and he was able to watch surfers competing in a modest surf while pelicans and helicopters flew overhead.

"How did we get here?"

"I seriously thought you wouldn't show up for a bit. In answer, we came by shuttle bus."

"Of course, I'm aware of that but the question is 'how did we get here to now'?"

"You mean, how did we come to be standing on a beach in Florida on a long cruise?"

"Yes, exactly!"

Watching the trim young bodies of high school boys and girls dressed in shorts or swimwear he contemplated the question. It had been in his mind a few times particularly over the initial part of the journey. He realised that there were two parts to this — the first biological, and the second environmental.

His thoughts focussed on the first. The teenagers on the beach oozed attractiveness, but in exactly the way it had happened to him, there had to be the actual attraction between a girl and a boy to trigger the possibility of reproduction. It was rare, and most of the people on the beach would never connect, in exactly the same proportions no doubt as most of humanity at large. Even then, the randomness of enormous numbers of sperm producing one winner that would fertilise an egg at precisely the right moment in the female cycle was such a chance process it appeared at best wasteful and at worst ineffective. Added to that, not all fertilised eggs turn into a healthy living baby.

To compound that, the years of human fertility are limited, not everyone is heterosexual, and not everyone is fertile.

As a method of producing additional human beings it doesn't look like a good solution, he thought. Evolutionists suggested that this randomness of choosing a partner ensured that healthy attributes were passed on because of the random selection from the enormous variety of the genes in the total gene pool. Maybe his terminology was a bit wrong, but his broad understanding of the theory was about right.

One problem. His understanding was that the whole of humanity started with three ladies from the Great Rift Valley in the middle of Africa a good many years ago. It followed that there must have been a few guys on the scene too, but the numbers would also have been very limited as must have been the opportunity for attraction or otherwise. For example, unkempt hair and beards (both sexes), long nails and chipped nail varnish, and a distinct lack of deodorant and perfume. He could imagine "I don't fancy yours much" on both sides and so no doubt a few prehistoric lagers may have been needed. In any event, it still equated to serious interbreeding from then on — there was simply no new blood if the start point was only, say, six individuals.

The next question was, given these inefficiencies and conflicts why are there two sexes? Not three or one, for example. Lots of things appear to get by with one sex only and some can even change sex when the mood takes them. They all manage to reproduce so it obviously works. The idea of three as a possible number was considered by him only to test out the concept, but the logistics would be interesting since getting two people to be attracted is hard enough so that finding a third would be a nightmare. Who would initiate the opening chat-up line — the female, the male or the other sex, or both, or even all of them? It was already difficult enough. The expression "three's a crowd" sprang to mind. Whoever wrote that must have given it a whirl.

Moving even further on with all this illogic, he wondered a number of other slightly connected thoughts, for example why don't humans have a pouch like a kangaroo? It would save parents from serious back

153

injury carrying little ones on shoulders or in the arms, and reduce the cost of children's clothing as they'd be kept warm so close to mother or father, depending on which had the available container.

And why do married couples often complain so much about their partners? Isn't that a bit like admitting to being an idiot because of who you chose to marry, and more of an idiot for staying that way?

And divorced people assuming it will be easy to find another perfect partner from a selection of those who have either never tried to be one or already failed at the attempt?

And why live births, when maybe laying an egg and leaving it buried in warm sand on a tropical beach or passing it to the male to tuck between his feet and look after would be so much easier. Or what about spawning and fertilising eggs in vast numbers like fish!? On consideration perhaps not the greatest idea and where might this take place — Glastonbury at one end of the scale, or Ascot for example at the other?

And why is self-pleasure frowned upon when the reality is that the process is designed to be pleasurable and the odds are that it was highly unlikely it was ever going to become a baby without a partner of the opposite sex being involved.

And why is protected sex considered bad by some when the people most involved may not actually want at that time to produce a baby because it would mean having to find money to bring up said baby perhaps by stopping working or giving up the satellite TV subscription, for example?

And why go through all the trouble of creating a living being when it will slowly start to break down and ultimately pack up altogether? Ageing and death are not inevitable if cells could continue the process of replacement. There are creatures who can supposedly live forever. He thought lobsters were one, but that immortality had sadly been destroyed for some of them for his enjoyment at the dinner table on this cruise.

He had real trouble fitting any sort of creator into all of this and the idea of some great plan, even a chance one, didn't hang together for him very well.

"Oh boy, that's really heavy. You OK?"

"Thanks, I'm fine but I can't help noticing things sometimes."

"Told you before, focus on getting a life."

"Supreme irony! That was all about new life."

"Not what I meant, and you know it. See you soon."

The weather had become cooler and he returned to the boat to sit on his balcony. He had already checked his emails and Sofia had made contact to say that her meetings had gone well, there was a social dinner and then early flights tomorrow to get home. She would contact him again when she was there. She was busy but missing him. He replied the same and told her that he looked forward to hearing of her safe return and that he would ring her the next day as he missed her voice.

He fell asleep in his own arms.

Day 64

32.4 degrees North, 79.4 degrees West

Total nautical miles travelled by midday — 18,641

He stretched his arm out in the bed and found nothing and then he woke fully to the realisation again that he was alone. No doubt he would get used to this soon, as he had been told. He showered and dressed. From the balcony, the sea was totally calm, a flat reflective mirror of water with striations of glossy smooth surface among the dimpled slightly darker water. He knew the Atlantic well. This was extremely unusual and spellbindingly beautiful. The sun was warm and the light breeze soothing. A number of dolphins appeared at intervals bouncing in the bow wave as they surfaced and dived and then swam towards the side of the boat as it passed, showing the white of their markings flashing several feet beneath the clear blue sea.

He felt special to be able to witness this. She would have adored it.

The journey along the east coast of America would take them to Charleston where they were due early afternoon for an overnight stop.

Entering the navigation channel to the port, he could see rows of doubtlessly very expensive beachfront houses built on stilts on the long sandy beach and facing the ocean. A low rock breakwater sheltered the channel with some red navigation buoys chiming melancholically as they rocked in the low swell, making a flat unmelodic sound. A solitary dolphin surfaced and dived a few times before disappearing behind the ship, and a sleek cabin cruiser raced past with no passengers other than the driver and a bag of golf clubs resting at the back. Some way to get to the golf course, he thought.

Minutes later a US Coastguard dinghy powered to the side of the boat. A machine gun was mounted at the front, manned by a man wearing a shiny blue helmet, blue clothing and an orange life jacket. It seemed unlikely that there would be either smugglers or pirates on the liner nor illegal immigrants, so this was probably just a show of force and as this it certainly impressed.

And then two more dolphins, light grey-coloured and swimming close together surfacing and diving briefly near the boat and possibly checking out this new arrival in their river estuary.

They docked and he went ashore walking around to get a feel of the city. It was elegant and seemingly very wealthy as attested by the builder's signs on properties being renovated and real estate agent's window displays. The city was a charming mixture of architecture with painted houses, shuttered and often gated with black ironwork. Several buildings had shaded courtyards with mature trees flanking many of the streets. A number had gas lamps by their front entrance doors, grand pillared balconies, flowering window boxes, and small alleyways. The shops and galleries were expensive, but the overall feel was charming and relaxed.

The vehicles, however, were another matter as many were monstrously sized pickups or four-by-fours, completely out of keeping with the ambience of the genteel city. At the other end of the scale, he saw a pushchair being wheeled along by a couple, and in which a dog sat happily. He did not think the expression about taking a dog for a walk meant this. Perhaps the dog was disabled. If not, the lack of exercise was not going to help in keeping it healthy.

Tired, he had coffee and a quite wonderful slice of moon cake containing marshmallows and chocolate, then enquired about the location of the restroom. The door was clearly labelled for men, but the toilet and washbasin were pink. He double-checked the sign, but it was correct. Was this how they did things in Charleston? Was this a form of southern charm?

In the evening he went ashore again, this time with friends from the boat. He ate exquisite oysters and seafood and drank good wine before returning to sleep as rain started to fall. If oysters were indeed an aphrodisiac the effect that night was totally wasted.

There was an email from Sofia in transit at Heathrow as she waited for her flight home. All was well, she missed home and sent love. He tried to call her mobile phone but she did not answer and so he left a long message and fired off a quick email reply to let her know before crashing out.

Gentle thoughts of her flitted through his dreaming.

Day 65

32.4 degrees North, 79.5 degrees West

Total nautical miles travelled by midday — 18,648

He had intended to spend more time ashore in Charleston before the departure in the early afternoon but the weather was cold, wet and grey and so he did so only briefly in order to check emails ashore. Sofia was home and promised to write more soon. He emailed her at some length about his activities, reiterating that he missed her company and conversation as well as her touch. He looked forward to being with her again for longer times when he got home too.

They sailed for Bermuda as the wet weather started to clear and he watched the passage away from Charleston along the lengthy marked channel and out to sea. It was cooler, and so he lazed watching a film on TV before dinner, a show and bed.

This, he reminded himself, was a replay of life before their meeting and although he had been happy this way before, it now felt very empty without her. When she was there the world was brighter in colour, his vision sharper and more focussed and life was seen in sparkling clarity as though an invisible gauze filter had been removed from his eyes. There was music everywhere, somehow, and in everything and he moved to its rhythm while his heart felt lighter and he floated seemingly weightless in his new sense of the present. Now was more now than before and he was more him.

"What is this thing called — love?"

"You may actually be right."

"Believe me, I am very, very right. You've definitely got it."

"If you say so."

"I just did. See you!"

He called her mobile phone and she answered. They had a long conversation about unpacking and getting washing and housework done, and he told her some of the things that had happened since she had left. But mostly they spoke about inconsequential things just to hear each other's voices. And about feelings, and missing each other's touch and caresses, and their desire to be together soon, and then goodbyes and blown kisses.

He slept very well.

Day 66

32.2 degrees North, 72.4 degrees West

Total nautical miles travelled by midday — 19,017

He woke several times during the night as the pitching and rolling of the boat was becoming quite strong. In the morning as the sun rose ahead of the ship, he could see the heavy seas being driven by a following wind. The horizon through binoculars was a ragged line of wave crests and white tops.

This was to be a long day at sea. He attended a lecture after breakfast and then watched the sea from his cabin.

He remembered that he had still to address the second part of the existence conundrum: i.e. the environmental reason for his being here.

"Thought you'd forgotten that."

"No, you wouldn't let that happen, would you?"

"Exactly. I'm a sort of failsafe device in your memory."

"So that I don't forget."

"Forget what? Just joking. Must fly, bye."

He contemplated again, as he had done so many times before, exactly what the key ingredients were in the making of him as who he now was. What recipe had been followed and by whom? Or was it, as his mother used to say 'I feel it in my bones', more probable that a great number of random constituents had been slung together over considerable time into an enormous blender, to be activated whenever a new bit of something relevant or important was located and added to the mix?

He knew very much who he was, but he also acknowledged that it was not who he had started out as. He had metamorphosed from small child to somewhat bigger adult in more ways than merely physical size. Unquestionably, parental influence had been strong, but it was hard to recollect which events had contributed the most. Which stories, happenings, rules, day-to-day occurrences, wise counsel or simple love and affection had done it? He knew that he would never really know but the thought process made him realise how much he had simply taken for granted as, he believed, all children must do. They can't sit around or hold up growing up to say things like 'Thank you, Mum, for bringing to my attention that hanging around with bad company is not likely to produce a good outcome, that saving for a rainy day is a terrific idea, or that becoming a slave to following fashion means that you will always be chasing something elusive while you go broke in the process.' It simply is not how it's meant to be and the occasional 'Nice lunch, Mum' is probably about the norm.

There were, however, some memories that stuck so strongly they were permanent. Many of them featured pets or special toys he had owned. Where did they go and what happened to them? He would often see things in shops and realise that he used to have one but didn't know where or when it had ceased to be in his possession. Some memories were so strong that the sight of an item would bring back instantaneously a taste, a smell, or a recollection of a shade of colour. And the feel of a fabric, for example, could do the same. He knew this effect from the failed business idea but when it happened for real it was such a powerful catalyst.

In terms of life experiences, there were only a few. At a very early age, maybe three or four, he had ridden his tricycle to a local park to sleep beneath a large low hanging bush. He could remember doing it but not any reason. He just wanted to do it. The result was a terrified mother thinking she had lost her small child, a police search and, for him, a ride home in a shiny black police car with a bell they rang to entertain him. Everyone had been very nice and very relieved. To him, it was just an adventure and possibly influenced some future life decisions. Or maybe not?

What was clear to him was that life had been good, and he had a tortoise. It followed therefore for his future that if things weren't too good the answer would be to get another tortoise. Thankfully, it had not yet ever been necessary.

One event had boosted his confidence enormously. A completely chance happening at school in his early teens when life was highly frivolous. The biology master was small, smelt of smoke, sported an evil moustache and a black gown stained by white and green chalk (or was it the mould of some decomposing dissected creature?) If he had been found to have conducted experiments on first year children, the older boys would not have been surprised. The reality was that he created so much fear in every class simply by his demeanour that there was no need for cruel experiments. His snarl, nastiness and throwing hard items at pupils maintained a high degree of discipline and when that failed, he would cane or slipper boys in front of the class.

At the start of one lesson, this biology teacher recapped the events of last week's lesson to the class. He had discussed he said, "Blah, blah, and blah. Wasn't that right?" The class response was affirmative. Marcus had doubts. "And we went on to learn about more blah, more blah, and more blah. Wasn't that right?" Again, the class response was affirmative, but Marcus could not hold back.

He knew that there was serious risk to him, but he said, "No, sir," as the class audibly drew in their breath. They expected blood.

"What do you mean 'No, sir'?" the teacher said with menace and a cruel glint in his eye as he fixed his gaze on his offending pupil.

He repeated, "No sir," and added, "we didn't talk about that. We talked about other blah, more other blah, and yet more other blah." And then he waited for the teacher's fury and a flying missile to hit him on the head, or at least a serious slap from the teacher for his insolence. But he knew he was right, and he'd had to say it whatever the consequences. Why? He was right and that was it. He just 'felt it in his bones'. If he'd been wrong, then that expression of his mother's would have been physically accurate, and he would have had serious pain in his joints and/or skull.

The teacher glowered, but not at him. Instead the rest of the class received the venom of whatever motivated this individual. Basically, he said that he had been talking balls although he did not use that word but rather the biologically correct one. He had been talking scrotum. He paused and reverted briefly to teacher mode — the plural of scrotum is scrotums he informed them and everyone had listened until one boy, just one boy, had shown even bigger scrotums in challenging him. One boy only out of thirty plus boys had dared to speak out. And that boy had been right. He had more scrotums than the rest of the class put together.

It was not a good mental image. All the rest were sheep with no scrotums whatsoever. Pathetic, or similar words of disdain.

To what extent that lesson had any impact on the rest of the class he had no idea, and nothing changed in the behaviour of the master or the other boys, but he had discovered something very powerful that he would use many times in his life. The truth should be defended.

Whether it was the influence of biology lessons, the look of the stockinged girls on the bus from the neighbouring girls' school, or just teenage hormones, the reality was that he and his friends found distractions that placed schoolwork well down the list of importance. They were all acquiring sex drives and for some the description sex overdrive would have been more appropriate. They were on a quest for discovery and this manifested itself in a natural curiosity about female anatomy. Had this been a subject on the school curriculum, they would have spent hours studying and achieving exam distinctions. It was not, and so they clubbed together any spare pocket money and took the train to Brighton where, near the station, they had learned of an interesting bookseller. It was a suitably seedy dark shop, but they were pleased to have found it. They scanned the shelves and searched for something affordable, appealing to all of them, and small enough to conceal on the return journey and in their bedrooms. In this Dickensian looking dark and dingy cave of a bookshop, they had stumbled not onto leather-bound first editions but upon the far more interesting (to them) concept of 'pocket magazines' which were aimed at discerning gentlemen.

They quickly perused the large array of tempting choices on the shelves. It was clear that browsing was not welcomed in this establishment. Reaching consensus, they purchased two magazines and tossed coins to determine in what order they would take them home for quiet reflection. That agreed, they scanned them furtively in the railway carriage as they headed back. Despite their supposed ignorance of such matters, they all knew somehow that the amply bosomed ladies pictured therein were not representative of ladies at large.

"Another Freudian slip — ladies at large/amply bosomed?"

"Not intentionally."

"Absolutely — that's the 'slip'. I'm off again."

And, worse — they had no genitalia. Nothing. A blank no-go area greeted their gaze. Plain and blank. They felt cheated. It was unjust that a censor somewhere, presumably in Whitehall was paid to look at photographs of ladies and then to decide that it would be in some way damaging to other men to see the same thing. What right did he have and how could they get a job like that? What a waste of their money. For the first time in their lives they felt cheated by authority, and the bookseller. Would this prove to fuel his rebellious anti-establishment streak? Or increase his curiosity? Possibly both.

It was soon after this that the school moved to new buildings necessitating a train journey. The fertile imaginations deprived of any sexual outlet focussed instead on clever ideas. This was an indicator of how Marcus's entrepreneurial skills would develop. The second-class carriages were too crowded with other schoolchildren and commuters. They should not have to tolerate such discomfort. First-class carriages, by comparison, were less crowded and often had individual compartments seating eight people and with no connecting corridor. The local education authority was, of course, driven by cost and did not think it necessary to provide first-class travel for teenage schoolchildren. Marcus did not agree. Neither did his friends.

He realised that it was possible to purchase an 'open' first-class return ticket valid for three months for a quite modest sum. When he explained how this might be useful, his friends agreed and so the group of six boys travelled daily to and from school in first-class carriages. Sometimes they were challenged by older businessmen to whom they proudly showed their first-class tickets. The stunned reaction alone was a delight and well worth the fare. On the very rare occasions that a ticket collector boarded the train, they surrendered the ticket and then simply bought another, in the process starting a new three-month period.

The trick was in entering and leaving the station. That required the school issue season ticket. The three-month return ticket stayed in their pockets.

In later life, he realised that this had been wrong on some level, but it was difficult to work out who had suffered from the actions. Nobody had been deprived of any property, the train had the seats available and was going on that journey anyway, and they behaved impeccably as would any first-class passenger of that era. He was just glad he didn't have to run that argument by a court of law and that it was not necessary to disclose any wrongdoing on a future job CV.

The group of friends were creative, and they enjoyed words. Disconnected thoughts flowed and from to time one of them would chip in with a gem of wisdom. He could still remember a few. 'Prostitution — where the customer always comes first.' 'Plagiarism — the sincerest form of flattery.' 'Oral sex sucks.' They were new to them and they enjoyed having created them.

And they loved hearing about a very attractive but none too bright girl who had apparently talked openly with the other girls about 'her Virginia'. How they longed to visit that Deep South.

Marcus also used words in his exams, inventing such phrases as 'Einstein is attributed as having said'. He calculated that a) it was unlikely the examiner would actually check provided that the quote sounded reasonable and b) it couldn't be wrong because he didn't say Einstein had actually said that, only that somebody had said that he had said it. It seemed that it had worked as he was never challenged, and he continued to use it in his work life too when required.

Was this evidence of a misspent youth he had wondered?

"Given the fact that many kids are now almost illiterate, you could have some fun and say 'mis-spelt youth'."

"Yes, I could, but I don't think I'll bother, but thank you."

"The pleasure is all mine. Must run."

The thrill of the chase evaded them all for some time so far as sexual experiences went and he would later on describe his life then as being like a growbag of un-germinated seedlings in an unheated polytunnel. It was a bit contrived but fairly accurate as the growth and blossoming occurred later.

Back in the present day, the Atlantic continued to behave roughly as expected, that is being rough. It must have been having a day off when it was flat calm a few days before. He went onto the rear deck, which was moving side to side and up and down. There was a small bird, possibly a sparrow, hopping around beneath the furniture which was lashed down for safety. It was more than three hundred miles to the nearest land, and he was concerned for it. If it made it to Bermuda, would there be any of its kind to welcome it? He found a potato chip on the floor, broke it into tiny pieces and threw it near the bird. The second time on the journey that the welfare of a bird had concerned him.

Sofia called him that evening and brought him up to date on progress on the negotiations for her project, which sounded positive. She would know finally in the next week or so. She missed him and was quite clear about what specifically she was missing at that time. He promised to make good when they met in Copenhagen in a few weeks. They must, they agreed, fix the dates and book his flights. He would do that immediately he got back home to London. More inconsequential talk, more about their feelings, and then fond farewells.

He slept that night in a bed that rocked and twitched in the sea as the propellers made odd vibrations throughout the vessel when the waves lifted the ship near the ocean surface. It was not a good night's sleep and predictably he missed her being close to him. Even if she had been there, it would not have improved his sleep.

But that was not the reason for wanting her there.

Day 67

32.1 degrees North, 64.4 degrees West

Total nautical miles travelled by midday — 19,433

The sea calmed as they entered the shelter of the passage through the reefs to Hamilton, Bermuda. It was cloudy but dry and he went ashore after breakfast to see the island he had wanted to visit for some time and which they had by-passed on the outbound journey.

They had this time avoided the Bermuda Triangle which lay to the south-west. The ferry from the naval dockyard where they tied up took them across the Great Sound to the city of Hamilton. But, despite the name of this stretch of water, he heard nothing at all on the journey.

"You're pushing it again — Great Sound — no noise. I'm off."

On every headland and each ocean front was a very large property painted a pastel shade and in perfect condition together with manicured lawns and lush gardens. Everywhere appeared to be built on a grand scale and provided striking evidence of the vast wealth on the island. It was all extremely smart, but he was left with an impression of artificiality and show — all designer home magazines and appeal factor in absolute contrast with the Caribbean. His view was that real people didn't live here.

Unfortunately, time restricted him from seeing the rest of the island and so he wandered around Hamilton and returned by ferry to see the naval dockyard, full of historic buildings and charming in spite of the shops and galleries.

As they sailed away in the late afternoon, the sun shone and the multicoloured reefs were visible just beneath the surface of the clear water beside the long and twisting navigation channel. As the ship weaved its way towards open sea, he could see in the distance large breaking waves crashing dramatically onto the edge of reefs, on top of one of which stood a yellow lighthouse starkly outlined against the sky. The channel, however, veered back towards the island and passed close by a fort complete with cannons on a headland with turquoise sea very close to the shore with yet more houses. Another headland, this time rocky, and then the ship headed out to sea with another sharp turn.

He called Sofia after dinner and they chatted for some time before he headed for bed, hoping to dream of her.

Alone was OK, but together was so much better.

Day 68

33.2 degrees North, 58.3 degrees West

Total nautical miles travelled by midday — 19,761

The sea day on board was horribly empty. He missed her company more than he could have imagined, and he squandered a day by doing nothing productive. It occurred to him that he might not have been like this if he had not met her. And then he tried to erase that thinking from his mind. Meeting her had been the most wonderful thing to happen to him in years, a high point in his already elevated life and a thing to be celebrated not regretted. Particularly as he had not lost anything, yet.

The losses in his life had hurt in different ways. Financially, when his bank went down with a lot of his money on board. He had the lifeboat of the few rental properties, and the rise in housing prices over the years had been kind to him, so that he had been able to liquidate these to buy his Battersea apartment with no mortgage and a comfortable sum of cash now in investments and an assortment of banks, protected by investor protections courtesy of the UK government. The property selection had also been helped by being able to buy the right thing at the right price during his days working in an estate agency and the timing of purchases during a slump in property markets. As a result, the pain of the financial loss had eventually been overcome.

The loss of wives and other meaningful relationships had left scars emotionally. He found them hard to identify unlike physical scars that could be seen, but they were there, and they had since then impacted on his ability to trust. Until now. Why was this different, and why had he let go of his mistrust and almost literally fallen into something alien to him for so many years? His only answer was that it felt right. So very right that his real fear was that just maybe his trust may have been misplaced and too hasty.

The scar that would never leave him was cut deep into his inner core, into his soul if such a thing existed. He did not like to think too long about the death of his young son. It was an abomination, an event which should never have been allowed to happen in any humane universe, so that the fact was that it had also destroyed his view of just, fair, reasonable, kind and any other similar adjectives.

It could also be loosely described as a loss when his seafaring days came to an end. Certainly, it was a loss of a cash income as well as his salary. It also unfortunately coincided pretty much with the bank failure and that partial loss of his wealth. It was occasioned by an unexpected request to meet with the personnel manager. Her title changed shortly afterwards to director of human relations, far more appropriate in these circumstances.

She was an older lady, much respected and not unattractive although they had done nothing more than mildly flirt at a couple of staff leaving parties. She did not mince words. She asked if he knew anything about a report of staff visiting passenger cabins against regulations. He replied "No" as he thought she was talking about other staff and he was obviously not about to acknowledge his own human relations venture nor drop any crew in the mire. Somehow, honesty seemed inappropriate in these circumstances. She looked him in the eye and said that specifically his name had come up. He asked who had made this observation, and he tried to look as innocent as he could even though he had no experience of having to adopt such a look.

She pointed out that he was employed to entertain guests. And that the entertainment was limited in his contract to singing for guests and dancing with them. She looked at him closely again and pointed out that it did not extend to horizontal dance movements. He thought momentarily that just maybe there was a hint in her eyes that she felt she had been overlooked in whatever had been going on. After a brief pause in which he remained silent, she told him that the information came from other than the staff or crew.

It was obvious to him that the secrecy the 'special' guests were sworn to had been breached somewhere. Loose talk had cost not a life but rather threatened his living. The cover it seemed was blown. He must protect the crew who had for so long laboured attentively providing pleasure to a select group of the lonely ladies and over so many years.

Satisfaction levels had always been high. Where had his quality control failed? How could this have happened? What must he do now? And what of his future?

He realised of course that the lady who had spoken out so indiscreetly had thought that it actually had been him in her cabin. He must maintain that illusion. In another stretch of his principle of honesty, he decided to resolve the problem by providing a degree of truth only. He agreed that he had indeed been very attracted to a more mature lady passenger and so had once only foolishly accepted her offer to a nightcap in her cabin, which had led to a little encounter between consenting people. It was, he repeated, a one-off event, it should not have happened of course, and he knew it was against rules, and it would certainly never happen again.

She said that she had heard his explanation and would record it as such in her staff files. She said that he was correct in saying that it would not happen again because she was now unable to extend his contract at the end of the current trip. He could stay until then as the ship needed the time to find a replacement. She regretted this but she had no choice given her position and said that she was sure he would understand that. At this point, she told him the formal and recorded part of the conversation was over. She hoped they could remain on good terms and that their friendship would not be affected. She suggested a quiet drink together in the nearest bar because it had been a difficult interview for them both. He accepted the offer and they moved to the bar where both ordered bourbon, hers on the rocks and his straight, and then chatted about this and that and some of the strange behaviour of guests over the years.

Finally, she said almost casually that she wondered how he had managed the arrangement with the passenger. He looked blankly at her and she continued. How had he arrived at getting a payment from the passenger when he had been so attracted to her? She reminded him that this conversation was off the record and she took a large swig from her bourbon. She then quietly and with perhaps a hint of a sparkle in her eye asked him to elaborate. She wanted to know, please, how he had managed to do this with two different lady passengers in different parts of the ship and, moreover, at precisely the same time on the same night.

He thought quickly and called on his creative mind. He must protect the other crew members — but how? Almost simultaneously the solution appeared. Perhaps, he ventured, one of the ladies had forgotten to change her watch when the time onboard was advanced. Nothing more was ever said on the subject, but he could not help thinking that the personnel lady had not quite bought his explanation. He was pleased that this part of the conversation was off the record.

He left with a clean reference and did a little travelling before returning to the UK where he lived a few weeks on his savings and rental income until he located work selling new build property in London. Docklands, the East End, Battersea and other areas were up and coming and the property market was fuelled by easy money courtesy of banks who could lend more against increasingly higher values of properties. Values rose as available mortgages increased, meaning that banks increased the amounts they could lend which increased their profits, buyers could pay more for a property aided by a higher mortgage, existing home owners borrowed more from the increased equity in their homes and spent it, and estate agents made more profit and were able to pay increased commissions and bonuses to employees like him. A win/win situation that could not fail. Until it did. But by then he had saved money, met his second wife and had two sons that he managed to educate privately.

Life continued to be good until divorce number two unravelled part of his wealth and some of his life. The job continued, however. He purchased a smallish flat and renovated it and was eventually able to rebuild his nest egg of savings and keep three rental properties that provided an increasing income until he sold them and his smallish flat to buy his newer and larger home.

And so, courtesy of a number of twists and turns in the highway of life, he was here now, and definitely at the high end of any satisfaction survey.

He would tell Sofia about the final twist in the onboard guest satisfaction business when they had more time. She knew everything about it other than the ending and he knew that she would find it entertaining.

She phoned him and they had their usual conversation about their day's events, ending with blown kisses. After dinner, he went to the Commodore Club for a nightcap and to listen to the pianist singing. The entertainment was good, as was the drink but it was a mistake because it made him more aware of her absence. There was nothing to do but take the air on the open rear deck for a few minutes and then get to his cabin to sleep.

"You're pining."

"Yes, I know, and I don't like it."

"Comes with the territory. It will get better. Got to dash again. Goodnight."

Day 69

34.4 degrees North, 50.1 degrees West

Total nautical miles travelled by midday — 20,186

It was a beautiful warm sunny day when he got up. The sea glistened silver with a long low swell gently moving the boat. They were in the middle of nowhere, mid-Atlantic with nothing to the horizon in any direction, a speck on the ocean, all at sea, a drop in the ocean and other similar nautical expressions. Plenty more fish in the sea again seemed at odds with the view of the vastness of water where once again no fish or creatures could be seen.

Although he was used to the sea from his former life, it was in the Caribbean always near to islands and he was working so that the current enforced inactivity for the few sea days was something he was unaccustomed to. Imprisoned, albeit in pleasant surroundings, but nonetheless unable to go anywhere except where the boat took him. At noon today came an announcement that they were 430 miles south of the wreck of the Titanic. Did it reassure people to hear that?

Maybe it was an age thing he thought but he hoped not, as he had always had a restless streak. The process of ageing was in evidence all around him on the boat. Often funny to observe but more often just sad. Funny watching an older person contemplating which yoghurt to eat, examining labels in successive identical pots until after some considerable time selecting one which was going to be the best to eat for some inexplicable reason apparent only to him. Sad to see people having difficulty walking particularly when the boat moved a lot. These people probably ran and played sport in their youth. And the other category for which the word sad was inappropriate where overindulgence had added such large amounts of flesh that they were now deformed and must surely have lost all self-respect years back. He acknowledged that he was prejudiced but he could not understand why people did not look after their bodies. My body is a temple appeared as a maxim to have been replaced by my body is a garbage dump.

"Sometimes, you can be really harsh you know."

"I tell it like it is."

"Thought you might have learned by now that it can get people into trouble."

"Yes, I realise that, but my problem is I was brought up to hold truth as a real value."

"OK, but just maybe that doesn't always work in this world. Got to go."

This world is he thought an interesting concept because it perhaps only exists in conscious thought. The world is only as we see and perceive it. Animals probably don't even contemplate it. The human animal is also supremely arrogant believing us to be at the top of some imagined pile or hierarchy, the superior species unrelated and disconnected from all other living things. But we still suffer the same ultimate fate of ageing and death. The problem is how we think about it and the fact that we can actually do so.

There is no vote about being created, no questionnaire or interview to inform the new potential being what it is going to be like becoming alive. No explanation that for many it will be a harsh existence filled with poverty, hunger, disease and suffering for the luckier ones, or with slavery, brutality, torture and maiming for the less fortunate. With only a very long-shot chance of being born into a vastly better life because the particular egg and successful sperm belonged to privileged parents. So much for truth, honesty and transparency except, of course, that there is no way to pose these questions to a pre-conception nonentity.

And then what about life chances like nutrition, health, good parents, education, environment? Little choice in those too. Even bright people ignore the best attempts to provide them with opportunities to develop, grow, and better their lives. Too many in the developed world expect a lucky break on some talent show from which they may, if lucky, get a few months of fame or money.

Throw into that the fact that after a certain age even those who have avoided chance illnesses will start gradually to deteriorate and fall slowly apart. In these situations, the luckier ones die before ageing catches up with them, while others become shunted into care homes until their savings are siphoned off. Or world cruises. The best hope there is to spend time sniffing lines of Lemsip with fellow souls or to take an overdose of rice pudding. Failing that dementia might help soften the harsh boundaries of the surroundings as, for example, on board where without fail each and every morning some people could be heard pointing out to their partners that they could see the sea. Their surprise should have been a delight to hear but it wasn't.

So, no vote on joining the party and no way of voting on how to leave and certainly no vote on it being a one-way ticket to oblivion. Who would vote to go on a trip like that? He had no complaints about his life journey — it had been wonderful so far, but he certainly was not pleased with the idea of being dead and he wondered who to complain to.

"Oh boy, you're getting worse."

"Just getting it off my chest."

"That should be brain not chest that you're getting it off."

"But you must admit I have a valid point."

"Yes, agreed, it's pretty hard for me to be independent minded in the circumstances as we are of the same mind. No point in me wasting energy arguing. I'm off."

Back in the real world of his cruise the sun shone more warmly, and he spent time mid-afternoon in the hot tub mid-Atlantic in mid-March. How crazy was that? Perhaps somewhere one of his gods was responding to his views on life and death and not merely smiling but laughing out loud?

The hot tub was also a conversation point that evening when he spoke with Sofia. She laughed and asked if it had been a hot tub of vice. He said that he thought she meant hotbed rather than hot tub and that it hadn't been as he had been in it alone. She indicated that she would find a private one when he came to stay with her and that she would do everything in her power to have it live up to her description. He responded that he thought that was a wonderful idea and would imagine it often.

Returning home was now becoming very much a reality and, in some ways, it was exciting to think about being back. More exciting was the thought of flying soon after to Denmark to be with her again.

Unknown to him as he fell asleep that night, there would be a change he could not possibly have anticipated.

Day 70

36.1 degrees North, 41.3 degrees West

Total nautical miles travelled by midday — 20,613

Gentle seas and warm weather again as they progressed steadily towards home.

He had a quiet day watching lectures and walking around the ship. He decided to email his children again as he had been regularly doing during the voyage, sending some pictures of interesting things or places. This one was different. He wanted to tell them about Sofia in preparation for introducing her to them after his return. It would be in some weeks' time because they had yet to plan her visit to him in the UK but it felt right to do it. It was important to him to let the children know.

"You sure about this? Remember going public on stuff before only for it later to fall apart?"

"I did worry about it, but it feels like the right time to do it."

"Your call. Just saying to be careful. Got to run, bye!"

There was a part of him that really did feel insecure about this relationship. It had been so sudden. It was joyous but it had been such a short time. Could it really continue that way? Was he fooling himself to think that it could last? His past life held harsh lessons for him about expectations and realities.

But surely this was just a symptom of them being apart, of not being with her, of no longer having the immediate and real confirmation of their love from her look, her touch, her kisses, and their shared intimacy? He hoped so. He really did. He must put these thoughts behind him.

It helped later when they spoke by phone and he heard her affirmation of her feelings for him and when he was able to again tell her his feelings but with no mention or hint of insecurity.

Before that, in the afternoon there was a diversion. He met people who told him that there was a dog onboard. A very small dog in a sort of handbag, its little head sticking out from the front of the bag carried over his shoulder by a male passenger. Bizarre. He would keep a look out for it.

He enjoyed another session in the hot tub before rain started in the late afternoon as a weather front caught up with the boat.

There was no sighting of the dog in the bag — a quick thought connection to the *Cat in the Hat* surfaced unexpectedly, followed immediately by Sofia's exquisitely surreal confusion with letting the cat out of the bag. He would never forget the pussy being completely out of the hat. How much he wanted her right now.

Dinner was pleasant with good conversation followed by the theatre and then sleep.

Unbeknown to him the plans for their meeting in Denmark were unravelling.

Day 71

37.2 degrees North, 33.4 degrees West

Total nautical miles travelled by midday — 21,006

He had overslept until late morning. The slow repayment of the extra hours that had been added going westbound was perhaps catching up as they were clawed back day by day going eastward. An announcement on the corridor speaker woke him. There was a gentle swell and the day was warm and sunny. In the distance was a big freighter going in the opposite direction against the swell making large white waves as the bow hit the oncoming sea.

At dinner last night, one of his friends on the table told him they had overheard a conversation that afternoon when someone reported hearing an American gentleman complaining to the Purser's office that the boat was rolling around. The response was not reported but they imagined it might have included reference to other vessels on the Atlantic moving similarly and the fact that this was not unusual, and had the passenger not heard about such things as waves?

It made him think that perhaps a guidebook to the oceans might have potential. After all there were so many city and country guides in book form and online that surely the sea must have some place in this information industry too.

"I like this idea."

"Great, let's put our minds to it."

"OK, I'll give it some thought. Just a bit busy now, must go."

He began the outline planning. Chapters and headings seemed easily to fall into place. Each ocean in turn, probably in descending size or maybe starting small and building up to create greater impact. Characteristics of each ocean by surface area, depth, volume, currents, undersea mountains and troughs, tectonic plates — all in detailed maps. The history of discovery and exploration and significant events like storms, shipwrecks, tsunamis, with features like tidal rises and falls.

Stories, myths and legends including sea monsters, the *Marie Celeste*, whirlpools, giant squid and so on.

In addition, some technical and interesting facts like degrees of wetness of the water in each ocean, salinity, buoyancy, temperature etc. He began to imagine the introduction:

'The oceans are extremely large and very wet, and they are filled with many different types and colours of water. Some are warmer than others and some are colder. Some even have ice. Man's ancestors crawled out of the oceans many years ago but lots of things didn't. There are a great many fish still left there. Some fish are not fish at all. They are mammals. While others are crushed asians (failure again of predictive text). Some creatures in the sea can be really big but some are so small you won't be able to see them so don't even bother looking. Most things can breathe underwater while others drown. Water has a thin crust called a hibiscus (predictive text again) that small insects can stand on. Birds have oily feathers so they can float. Boats have some other oily features, so they float. People sink if they can't swim even if they are oily. There are more oceans than land on the earth. Go and visit them before they get spoilt.'

He thought that was pitched about right for people like the American.

"Couldn't have put it better myself. I'm off to bed soon. Sleep well."

He rang Sofia and told her about the American. She was amused. Her day had gone well, and it seemed the film concept was looking very promising. She was very excited about it. He also mentioned the dog but said that he had not yet seen it. They talked at length about very little other than their wish to meet soon, and again their feelings. They were missing each other. The weather in Copenhagen was cold.

After the phone call he checked emails. The children each said in their ways that they were happy for him and wished him well. They looked forward to seeing him soon and hearing all about the trip.

A drink at a bar, dinner and conversation and then a show followed by bed and good dreams. Nothing to be concerned about.

Day 72

38.4 degrees North, 27.3 degrees West

Total nautical miles travelled by midday — 21,334

He awoke as they were about to enter the harbour at Praia da Vitoria, the Azores. He checked the geographic coordinates on the TV map and saw a straight black line showing their course since last night. It indicated that they had sailed right through two islands. That would have been very interesting, but he had slept through it.

The shuttle bus took him into the town for his second visit, this one planned unlike the emergency stopover early on the cruise, and he walked further than the last time. Having seen the town more fully he took a local bus to the city of Angra do Heroismo, a UNESCO world heritage site. The bus drove at speed through twisting lanes stopping frequently to load and unload passengers, and passing smallholdings with tiny fields flanked by rough stone walls. Everything was green and lush, and flowers grew profusely in the gardens of small properties. There were many cows and calves grazing and some being herded along the main bus route at one stage forcing the driver to stop. Generally, the bus driver behaved as if he was on the track of the Monaco Grand Prix, which the undulating roads in some ways resembled.

Many of the fields fell away to sea cliffs overlooking islands clearly of volcanic origin, stumps of vertical rock rising out of the sea. Other than that, he was reminded of the coast of West Wales although the walled fields were like those on his uncle's farm in Staffordshire many years ago. Everything here was small scale and charmingly old world.

The city was beautiful, the streets and squares cobbled and patterned, and the buildings elegant often with balconies and carved stonework many dating back centuries to the great ages of early world trading. Vasco de Gama had sailed from here in 1499 on a voyage of discovery and there was a rich history of both trade and conflict. His time however was limited by the need to get back on board by late afternoon ready for an early departure for home.

It started to rain as he boarded the ship for the last time. In a few days' time in Southampton he would finally leave her.

The evening followed the now established pattern with another long phone call this time from Sofia. No new news but all was well, and time was passing quickly so that it would not be long now until they met.

He really hoped so.

Day 73

41.4 degrees North, 21.2 degrees West

Total nautical miles travelled by midday — 21,653

When he rose, there was a long low swell, with overcast but mild weather. They were level with Lisbon in Portugal but well to the west, making good progress towards Southampton.

They had changed captain before leaving the USA and the midday message about position and weather had developed a new aspect with the addition of a jokey thought for the day at the end of the broadcast. Previous ones had been corny but today's was a gem — "If at first you don't succeed then freefall parachuting is not for you."

The day was uneventful, the evening spent like others but there was a show with four rock musicians that had the theatre almost full, with people standing and dancing at the finale. It was a wonderful end to an otherwise ordinary day. The feeling of pleasure was added to by his late-night conversation with Sofia. He came off the phone longing to see her soon. The days were flying by on one level and he now just wished to be home and to make arrangements for his visit to her.

"I can sense anxiety about you being apart and trying later to reconnect."

"You're very observant. I was trying not to think about that."

"You do realise it may not turn out as you anticipate?"

"Which way?"

"Either — better than you think… or not."

"Wish you hadn't brought that up."

"Oh, well. Can't help it. Tell it like it is. Good night."

He had difficulty shaking off the thought and it was a long time until he got to sleep.

Day 74

45.2 degrees North, 13.6 degrees West

Total nautical miles travelled by midday — 22,043

They had passed the north-west corner of Spain in the night and were into the Bay of Biscay, notorious for vicious stormy seas. Like the Atlantic before, it too was having a relaxing day and not doing much. The sea had a slight swell only, the cloud was high, and the sun breached it from time to time creating a silver glow on a thin sliver of sea towards the horizon.

At breakfast he observed people getting food and going to and from tables. There was a feeling of fatigue he thought. Warmer duller clothes were in evidence, contrasting with the bright colours worn in the tropics. People were ready to be home.

He was becoming bored. Perhaps he should have flown back from the Azores to avoid the last few days at sea. The reason he was still here was because he had anticipated rough and stormy seas. He really enjoyed the wildness of the weather, the view of the churning ocean, and the challenge of moving around the boat together with the camaraderie of other guests who enjoyed it similarly. It was unfortunate for people who did not travel so well but they generally knew the risk and it was not therefore anything he needed to feel bad about.

As it happened, and despite the disappointingly calm seas, it turned out to have been a good decision to stay onboard.

He wondered why people went on long cruises. The appeal of seeing new places on holiday while being waited on hand and foot was understandable and had considerable appeal. But the sea days had a serious downside for him. It was like being in a good hotel overlooking the sea with great service and food where entertainment was laid on. But movement was restricted, and it was only permitted within the confines of the hotel itself. It was not possible for several days at a time to go anywhere else. He had little doubt that most people did not mind this but for him it might influence thoughts of future lengthy cruising.

Late afternoon he saw the small white dog in the bag. It was not in a dress as somebody had said they'd seen it some days before. It did not however seem interested in him and so he passed it by. It was also not at the captain's final formal cocktail party but plenty of fizzy wine, red wine and caviar was. He was much more interested in those.

He and Sofia spoke as usual by phone but there was little news from either of them, so they just talked and reminisced a little. After dinner he went with some friends from the table to the Commodore Club for drinks. For him the memories here were strong and he passed some time chatting about the voyage and people's next trips and holidays. The friends already knew that he planned soon to see Sofia in Copenhagen.

They too could not know it would not work out like that.

Day 75

49.0 degrees North, 6.0 degrees West

Total nautical miles travelled by midday — 22,428

It was the final day of the voyage. Tomorrow early morning they would be in Southampton and he would go home, there to make plans to visit Copenhagen.

"Don't know about you but I'll be glad to get off this boat. Far too restricting. See you later."

At breakfast he sensed the mood of people being ready to be home. The captain walked around chatting to everyone in his positive and cheerful way, presumably taking the pulse of final feelings but also socialising and making people feel important.

Back in his room he packed two large suitcases surprised because he fitted everything in including a few acquisitions from the trip. He had been careful about buying too many souvenirs and was now happy at that decision having heard of a nearby cabin stacked with boxes of gifts.

The day was passed doing very little, filling the void in time until the arrival. Excitement at returning was replaced by just wanting to be back. It seemed a long crawl back up the English Channel with nothing to see except low grey cloud and the white caps of low waves.

He ate dinner for the last time, tipping the waiting staff and thanking them for their excellent service and he did the same with his charming and attentive cabin maid. That night was the final event in the ballroom with the rock band playing. He would love to have danced but the dance floor was very full, and he was reluctant to ask a stranger. His preferred partner was no longer on the boat. Instead he stood on the sidelines, quietly singing along.

The evening phone call with Sofia ended with them both saying how much they wished they could get together again very soon and that they would make arrangements when he returned home. Love and kisses were exchanged but they both wanted it to be face to face rather than remotely.

As he fell asleep, he contemplated bringing forward the arrangements for his trip to see Sofia — perhaps only a few days alone in the UK?

It was not, however, to be so.

Day 76

50.5 degrees North, 1.2 degrees West

Total nautical miles travelled by midday — 22,650 and the end of the voyage.

He left the ship early morning having waited for his turn to disembark. His suitcases had gone ahead last night to await collection in the terminal building. Nothing exciting, just getting back onto land ready to get a taxi to the station for a train to London. He located his bags and wheeled them outside towards where the taxis were waiting. There were so many people, so many bags and packages and so many vehicles.

Something tapped his shoulder and he thought it was an impatient passenger attempting to get to the taxis first. He ignored it, not wishing to lose his place in the long queue, but it was followed immediately by a stronger tap and a voice: "Looking for a good time, sailor?"

He turned quickly wondering if he had heard correctly. Sofia beamed at him and wrapped her arms around him giving him the tenderest of long kisses. He held her shoulders as he looked at her smiling.

"What are you doing here?" he asked and then kissed her.

"I thought I might find somebody interesting from the boat looking for a good time," she said "Trade has been very quiet for the last week or more. I thought you might be interested."

"More than interested," he replied, "I'd like to hire you for life. Can I afford you?"

"I think maybe there can be a special discount offer for returning sailors," she responded.

She had flown to London the evening before and had taken his phone call while she was at the airport, hoping hard that he would not hear the background noise of people. Then a bus and overnight at a small hotel near the docks to be ready for his arrival. She had found out his disembarkation time based on his cabin number. She was free to come with him to London if he would like that. He more than liked that as an

188

idea, especially when she said that she was free to stay several days so that maybe he could return with her when she went home.

They stood unmoving from the spot, holding, kissing, smiling and laughing for some time until they eventually moved to the taxis with his large cases and her one smaller suitcase, and having loaded their luggage, went to the station and took a train to London and then a taxi to his Battersea apartment.

As they entered, he apologised that he had not cleaned the place since the last lady had been there. He said this with a smile and when she asked how long ago that had been, he told her truthfully that it was many years. Her response was that he must live very tidily indeed or that maybe the last guest had not been very dirty. He took that remark at face value and did not elaborate on the possible alternative meaning.

They shopped for essentials and went for an early evening meal at his favourite local Chinese restaurant before heading back to the apartment and the warmth of the central heating that he had turned up on his return.

They sat together enjoying drinks before bed exchanging news about her project and his final cruise days, and then they reunited in bed.

Noting that absence did indeed make hearts grow fonder.

Day 77 onwards

He had no need any more to count the days. There was no reason. Each day was a delight as they spent the first few months finding out about each other's cities, their lives, their friends and families. He introduced her to his children and grandchildren over dinner in a smart restaurant and as he had anticipated they liked her and got on well. They met each other's friends and other relatives over dinners at their respective flats, or at restaurants and found all of them to be interesting and entertaining with a wide variety of interests and great senses of humour.

They planned holidays and trips in some cases linked to her work filming in exotic holiday places. Her role was to explore these and report on them from the perspective of a mature single female traveller. The end-user clients were an international travel agency who would be sponsoring the series of television programmes, as well as an agency planning to sell them to airlines and hotels etc. The agency had spotted a gap in the market and wished to promote holidays to the generally wealthy mature female sector of the public who were often uncomfortable travelling alone. It was perceived as a lucrative market sector if it could be tapped into successfully.

She was to portray a relaxed typical lady in such a situation who could share her enjoyment of the freedom of seeing new and exciting places on her own. This was not difficult as she was being paid to do something she loved anyway. No reference was made to the fact that she had a partner on her trips who shared evenings, dinners and her bed. It was not a part of the brief to refer to sexual opportunities for the single lady travellers although she was able quite naturally and for the camera to flirt occasionally with attractive waiters, tour guides, or smartly dressed elegant older gentlemen in hotel bars. The implication was that the ladies viewing might find success in that field if they wished to.

Suitable 'health warnings' were always given about reducing risk when travelling by avoiding certain areas, not wearing expensive jewellery or clothing, and being generally sensible. This latter caution always managed to imply that matters sensual were included in the 'being sensible' category, and she would sometimes say to lighten the message that in those circumstances, jewellery and expensive clothing were permitted when not outside in public spaces. Wealthy mature ladies, she was well aware, wished to feel comfortable about dressing well for dinner or drinks, and by implication undressing well if the circumstances allowed.

It was a fine line creating the message that older ladies were sexual beings too in the right circumstances and that they often viewed exotic holidays as being a stepping stone to finding physicality. Lonely people wished to find love again or at the very least to feel they were still attractive.

The filming was not challenging. They worked initially to get a few shows 'in the bag' and then filmed two or three new ones about twice a year. It was work she enjoyed, and she negotiated a reasonable fee that included the travel and hotel costs for them both. The films were drip-fed to the market and it was intended to continue them indefinitely as the potential locations were numerous. Within a few years, updates might also be needed.

They revisited some places from the cruise as well as some cities they both knew well and others that they did not know at all. It was a delight for her to work like this and he lost no opportunity to praise her skills and thank her for being with him. He decided to tell her his role was to be her bodyguard, because he liked nothing better in life than guarding her body, particularly in close proximity situations. She agreed readily.

The 'voice' was appreciative and put in regular but infrequent appearances. Apparently, it was quite occupied in creative work of its own, or so it said. He always told her when a meaningful observation came to him from the voice and they joked about it. Some people might think that they were in conversation with some spiritual being, a god, or the God of choice. There was plenty of evidence for that historically but the voice had never claimed anything along those lines, and he had no belief in such things so that it was unlikely he would be converted to some faith or other just because something chipped in from time to time with a thought, a criticism or an observation.

Had it sometimes been associated with a burning bush, a host of angels, a parting of the seas, or a really great light show he might have been influenced, but it was just a voice, more a friend and mentor than anything.

Together when not working, they explored London, Copenhagen and their own countries, mixing galleries, exhibitions, museums and shows with simply wandering back streets to make new discoveries. They were in total harmony and happiness and life was extremely good to them.

Birthdays clocked up with, it seemed, increasing frequency marked by cocktails, fine dining, family, friends, and increasingly silly cards.

Sofia frequently told him that his imagination was wild. Often this was after he had explained another of his entrepreneurial concepts. Perhaps the most interesting of these was his lottery idea.

There were, he knew, many people like him who regularly picked numbers that never came up. Not a single one. Mathematically the solution was obvious. Create a syndicate where a number of these people pooled their knowledge, picking their numbers as usual but then simply eradicating those from the available choices leaving a selection of potentially winning numbers i.e. those they had not chosen. If they consistently picked only losing numbers, then what was left must be winning numbers.

The brilliance was in the simplicity of the idea, but he never developed it because of the complexity of promoting it, and the costs of running it, plus he simply did not want to do it.

Instead he took the concept to the Roulette table at a local casino as part of a night out. They set a budget for that night's entertainment and sat at a busy table watching the other players who generally were losing consistently. He started to play, placing chips where the other players had not. Roulette is a matter of timing — lose quickly or lose slowly, with an occasional win that most people 'reinvest' only to lose quickly or slowly. His previous pattern had been rapid losing, but this time was indeed different.

Sofia played her own game while observing his. On her third bet with a not inconsiderably valued chip she picked 23 and watched as the ball bounced around and settled into that position on the wheel. The healthy amount of chips was added to her stake and she quietly slipped one to the croupier, collected the pile of her winnings, and went to cash them in. As she slid elegantly from her stool, he watched the male players observing her. He could see the desire on their faces, for her and/or for the money. Hardly surprising given her appearance and the amount she was taking from the table.

He made one more unsuccessful play and then gave up. The theory was not proving good. He was financially down but with Sofia's skills they were well in profit overall. They put the proceeds towards cocktails and dinner with a healthy surplus for future evenings out, and they could not stop laughing for the rest of the night. They kissed a lot and he told her again how much pleasure he had watching her and being with her.

"It doesn't feel right."

"What do you mean?"

"Something isn't as it should be, but I can't put my finger on it — at least I wouldn't be able to even if I had a finger."

"Nothing's wrong. It's your imagination."

"That's ripe — I am sort of your imagination."

"I thought you said you were my conscience, my alter ego or such."

"Correct, those things too but you have to believe me — something is not quite right."

"OK, just for the sake of the argument, what is it that makes you think that?"

"Told you, can't put my finger in it. Got to run."

A few days later he told her he had a strange sensation in his right hand. He thought he'd slept on it. A sort of numbness he said like pins and needles but not. It remained. About a week later, he dropped a spoon as he was eating dessert and they laughed as he had ice cream all over his shirt and trousers. But the laughter was anxious and when a similar thing happened again in another couple of days, they knew that they must check with a doctor.

An examination, some questions and a few basic tests led to the suggestion of a referral to a hospital for more detailed tests. He said that all would be well, and she smiled, although fear had now entered the playground of their lives.

She made exquisite love to him that night and he embraced her holding her tightly. He did not dare tell her that he could not feel the beautiful smooth skin of her back with some of the fingers on his right hand. He prayed to whatever he had no belief in that it would not last and that he would not be permanently robbed of the simple pleasure of touch.

"I've got it!"

"I think you'll find that I am the one who has it."

"Well then we both do but that wasn't what I was saying."

"Go on, I have time."

"It wasn't that I have the condition, whatever it turns out to be, it's that I have part of the solution."

"OK, carry on. I'm all ears even if maybe not all hands."

"Jelly beans."

"Run the detail of your thinking by me, please."

"You love them. So much so in fact that you've always avoided buying them too frequently because when you do buy them you devour whole packets as if you were addicted to them."

"True, and the same goes for chocolate as you know."

"Well then, a controlled dose of medicinal jelly beans will help you maintain your positive outlook because you'll always be wanting more of them! And that will keep you alive waiting for your next fix. Plus, they have so many good things in them."

"Full of preservatives I think you'll find."

"Exactly — they will help to preserve you, and the fruit extracts and sugars will give you lots of energy too so you can continue to enjoy life to the full."

"You're making a compelling case."

"Well, you could say that you just persuaded yourself, or maybe simply justified revisiting the pleasures of the jelly bean supported by reasoned argument."

"OK, I'm sold."

"Great, have to get on you know. Catch up soon."

He drove to a nearby shopping mall where he knew there was a large supermarket selling confectionary. He bought their entire stock of jelly beans, seventeen bags in total, and he placed an order for a large box full of each variety, Kids Favourites, Fruity Juicies and Sour Beans, to be collected by him within the week.

In the hands of an addict, he could easily overdose on sugar, fruit concentrates, and an assortment of food colourings but his intention was to remain alive and he would use self-discipline by locking these away until he discovered the nature of the ailment. Well, apart from six bags for measured consumption over the next week. Well, maybe seven bags to keep it simple. How would you apportion six bags over seven days anyway? Too complicated and he did not need any additional anxieties.

When it came to the medicinal use, he would enlist Sofia's help to administer the requisite dose at the correct times. He would consider exactly what this requisite dose constituted in the next few days when he knew more about the 'ailment'.

He looked forward to this part of any treatment and perhaps on occasions Sofia could be persuaded to truly enter into the spirit of the situation and wear a nurse's outfit. The thought cheered him, and he decided to ask her nicely over dinner that night.

Sofia agreed willingly to his suggestion but pointed out the need to ration the fantasy due to his obvious addictive tendencies. She also observed that she did not wish to add any complications to his existing health situation, whatever that might turn out to be. She was sure that increased blood pressure and too much excitement would not be good for him and would need also to be limited and controlled.

He pointed out that if they had been aware on their voyage of this health issue, they could no doubt have purchased a suitable uniform in the store selling the dentist chair and the other medical items. They would now need to shop online. They did so and were not surprised by the number of fancy dress and erotic costumes which vastly outweighed the real thing. For authenticity they purchased a real one and she seemed excited that they had achieved this.

They said little about their fears and passed the time until the hospital appointment enjoying life to the maximum. Dining out featured high on their activities, as well as the escape of cultural events, and just being together.

They could afford private treatment, but this still meant a short wait and then a series of blood tests, x-rays, and scans until eventually an appointment was arranged with a senior consultant after a few further days.

He continued to feel fine and kept reassuring her that he was sure there was nothing serious. "If there had been," he said, "they would not have allowed me to continue with my private nursing arrangement at home. They would have placed me in a bed surrounded by private nurses who would attend to my every need."

"Oh," she said, "I think there is one need at least that is done better at home."

Unexpectedly their closeness intensified during this waiting time, signalling the depth of their love and their wish for it to continue for as long as possible. They made light of their unspoken fears as if voicing them would give them life and reality. Trivialising the fears diminished them in some way.

The initial course of jelly beans commenced, overseen by Sofia, occasionally dressed as agreed, and she took great interest in the ingredients listed on the packets. The Nutritional Facts advised that twenty-seven pieces was a 'serving size' of which there were about nine servings to a packet. His daily sugar input would be 42% met by this and he would consume large amounts of fruit concentrate and puree, plus assorted acids, artificial and natural flavours and colours, and a number of odd things including beeswax. She had researched websites also and found that jelly beans were often coated with shellac which may well have been called something different on these packets. If it was, it could have been for good reason because shellac came, she had read, from beetle excrement from India and Thailand. When she had told him this, he thought it added to the exotic feel of his medication. He was sure the beetles would be pleased to hear that their waste products were being put to such good use. It might give them a sense of purpose.

He told her that he was fascinated by items he had read about the placebo effect. Fake drugs work effectively because the recipient believes in them. The best, however, was research where the fake treatment was revealed as a fake, but the patient still got better. He knew he was playing with that theory and that he was effectively deluding himself, apart from the very real benefits of the jelly bean ingredients and his enjoyment tasting them.

He told Sofia, in a jokey attempt to have her dress up more often, that the placebo effectiveness was also enhanced when the person handing out the fake drug dressed in a white coat. How much better, he had argued, that a proper medical uniform be used rather than an ordinary white coat that could belong to anyone? Her reply was simply that in her professional medical opinion he had an overactive imagination and that she might need to arrange for it to be surgically removed. As the words came out, she froze, realising that this could be horribly near the truth and that she may have hurt him. After the briefest pause he started laughing infectiously and they both continued for some time.

A few days later he visited the consultant alone. She understood that he would deal better that way with whatever he heard and would tell her when he had understood what there was to deal with. She would have wished to be there to offer support but had told him that she recognised why he had to do it that way.

The appointment was kept almost to the second. The sort of precision appropriate for a top consultant surgeon and what he had would have wished for. The results were outlined with great clarity and calm, as well as the proposed course of action.

He listened quietly letting the information sink in. In reality it more dropped in, displacing something as it fell, that is the equilibrium maintained by day-to-day living and the constant knowledge of our finality that we ignore.

He thought for a few moments and then broke the silence.

"I probably shouldn't ask this, but it seems to be expected in these circumstances... How long do I have?"

The response was slow and measured with eye contact held all the way.

"The rest of your life."

A brief pause.

"Something tells me that you aren't being facetious."

"One hundred percent correct. You are an intelligent person and I want you to understand fully the implications of the information I have just given you. The diagnosis is an opinion, a likely outcome based on considerable amounts of evidence and experience... but nobody can know what exactly will happen or how. To say that 'you have the rest of your life' is the only truth I can offer. It means that you should grasp that and live every moment as though nothing has changed. In many ways it hasn't. I just conveyed some information about one thing that may contribute to your death. There are a million others — accident, some other illness, natural disasters etc. and your death is sadly an inevitability as is mine and everyone's on this small planet."

"That's... extremely direct." He paused briefly gathering his thoughts. "And extraordinarily helpful... strange really in some ways, given the circumstances."

"I don't think it's productive to skirt around the issue with patients who can understand and deal with things. You know the score so you can choose how to live whatever time is left. Let me tell you what I propose that we do."

The use of the word 'we' was purposefully inclusive indicating that the solution required two active participants.

The consultant quietly detailed the course of his preferred action. He explained that the choice not to operate in the hope of removing the growth they had discovered was a balanced decision. Given its location the probability of total removal was limited. He might or might not be successful, and the risk of brain damage was very real. He would not give percentages but rather said that his professional view was that other treatment options were a better risk for a patient of his age. The growth might slow or even stop, particularly with the right treatment, and the side effects might not worsen or might proceed very slowly. Maintaining a close to normal life for as long as possible seemed to him preferable to taking radical action that could immediately destroy the quality of life or even kill him.

He then spent time outlining the limited range of other options, including chemotherapy and radiation treatment. He also explained that these might or might not produce any dramatic results but would certainly affect the quality of life in the short term at least. The desired outcome was not guaranteed but he suggested the cost/benefit equation could be workable. He initially recommended radiotherapy together with chemotherapy.

Finally, he asked quietly, "Is that all clear to you, do you have any questions, and are you happy to proceed? I have to say that if we are to do this, we should waste no time."

A further pause.

"Yes, no, and yes," was the response. "But I have to say that I shall also be using an alternative therapy alongside all this."

"I have no objection, provided it doesn't clash with my proposals. In fact, I welcome patients being involved. You are no doubt aware that recovery and survival rates are higher where people have a positive outlook. May I just ask what?"

He answered the consultant whose response simply was, "New one on me. Good luck. Be interesting for us both to see how it goes."

They shook hands having agreed the series of treatments and further appointments.

Returning to his flat, she was waiting. Although she had not accompanied him to the consultant appointment, she had been with him in thought. He had needed to maintain his full focus on what he had feared would be revealed and yet had somehow known. She had kept busy preparing a special dinner. They kissed and she asked how it had gone.

He told her the diagnosis and watched as she maintained her composure but with a tell-tale tear showing. As she hugged him tightly, he reminded her of his theory of positive thinking in health situations and told her again how he had fixed several health problems by thinking them away.

"Do you remember," he asked, "that holiday in the Canaries when I did something to my knee and couldn't walk? When the German looked at me shuffling along and asked 'Kaput?' My response of 'Ja' exhausted almost all my German vocabulary! I saw a specialist who proposed an MRI scan, but I thought that pointless other than that it would probably show some damage. I already knew that — my knee was telling me pretty directly in its own way. So, I just spent weeks thinking it better and it worked. There were other times too throughout my life when I managed the same results. Maybe these things would have got better anyway, who knows, and I'm convinced that this is no different, except this time I also need a bit more support."

She smiled and reminded him that she would also be his support.

"I don't know how I know this," he said, "but this thing is definitely not going to kill me." They could not then have known how true this would prove to be.

The treatment itself was not difficult to get on with. What was difficult was the knowledge that however precisely it was targeted, it could not be that focussed, and that damage was undoubtedly being done elsewhere than the growth. That was the nature of the beast and it took great positivity to remain comfortable with that. In addition, the side effects were extremely unpleasant making him tired and nauseous combined with simply feeling not at all good. He managed to joke that the hair loss would not be an issue as he had so little, although this was the only positive he could pluck from the situation.

But he knew that the treatment was relatively short, and the consultant was reassuring. He managed, mostly, to stay positive for Sofia's sake.

Finally, the tests at the end of the treatment revealed no significant change. The consultant pointed out that this was a good outcome — things had stopped or slowed down dramatically. He was to get on with life with a check-up in six months unless there was any deterioration.

The numbness persisted in his hand and more recently his arm, but it had not worsened, and he coped, by using his other hand when he could. That was not always easy particularly with writing, but Sofia said that his already dreadful writing could hardly get much worse.

The expression 'life goes on' was certainly totally relevant to them and they made many plans.

They agreed that so far as the rest of their lives were concerned that they were on a wild ride and would seek thrills and satisfaction wherever and whenever they could.

They travelled to places on their mutual wish list and to those on each other's lists. Beaches, cities, countries, cultures, people, experiences, food, drink, scents, sights, sounds beckoned everywhere. They knew that there were so many things that they could not do them all in a normal life. So, they decided to live abnormal lives and use these things as a justification for living many more years. 320 for him remained the goal with a review at that time and she bought in to the same timescale, although her planned method of departure did not include a Harley Davidson in the south of France or a tall woman. She said that maybe a tall man would be appropriate, perhaps in South American Indian costume, but that she would keep her options under review.

They revisited things that they had done before in their lives and tried everything new that they could find with very few restrictions. For him heights were not good, but they rode long zipwires, high cable cars and climbed tall buildings. It made him laugh that years back he would have gripped handrails or whatever to feel secure and now he could not feel the rail properly because of the lack of sensation in his right hand. No matter, he could see that he was holding on and that worked.

It was a joyous few years. His health had remained stabilised and his spirits were high because she was with him. They loved and lived in constant fun and laughter.

The voice maintained contact with regular comment and commentary. Although challenging at times it supported their positivity.

"We're in this together, mate," or similar was the usual tone.

In the Algarve on an idyllic holiday they both wanted to ride a horse in the sea again. It was something they had each done, years before they met, and the memory had stayed with them. Both had been capable riders. They booked at a local stable and met their guide and their horses; large, friendly and docile, named Fleur and Rosa.

The ride was wonderful, and they had not lost their skills. As he said, it was like riding a bicycle. She said, yes but without any need to pedal. Their ride took them through olive groves and then to a path above the coast. A short steep track led down to the small narrow beach with rough grasses, and the incoming tide lapping at the sand of the lagoon, with the long narrow stretch of beach opposite flanking the ocean. It was so quiet with the sound of birds and the absence of people that they christened it a little paradise and agreed that they would be back, possibly to walk the track as well as ride.

The guide told them about the area and the plants and animals. Seeing that they could handle the horses he asked if they wished to canter some of the return and they readily agreed. The guide led, with Sofia second and him following. They nudged the horses into action and rode happily with the sun and wind in their faces through the lapping water's edge creating splashes as they went. Their delight would have been obvious to anyone watching but there was no one else to see it.

It was never entirely clear what happened and why his horse may have stumbled and then reared and thrown him. Perhaps the flap of the sail of the single distant windsurfer on the open sea beyond the lagoon?

His hat was secure, and the wet sand was soft so that he did not break any limbs or sustain any damage to his head. Had he been able to, he would have said that the fall wasn't dangerous, just the last bit.

He lay on the ground motionless. There was no visible injury, but he remained completely still. His neck had broken instantly as he hit a lump of rock, invisible in the gently lapping water.

She and the guide saw his riderless horse pass them and turned back. It was immediately clear how serious this was. She dismounted, followed by the guide and went to his side. He seemed to have a large smile on his face, proof of the pleasure of the day and with no time in the instant of the fall to change his expression. She knew he was dead but checked for a pulse and put her face to his lips to see if he was breathing. The guide checked the pulse too and then held her and apologised as they both wept. A mobile phone call enlisted the help of medics for all that was worth to him. Before they arrived, she held his cooling hand and kissed him many times.

Had there really been a faint disembodied voice as she had knelt beside him or had she simply imagined the breathless, "Oh, fuck"?

"Not a motorbike or a tall woman," she whispered to him. "But maybe a good way to go without suffering. I already miss you and that won't get better. Thank you for everything you gave me in so many ways. It was indeed a wonderful pleasure to be part of some of your life. And you chose to die already in paradise."

In reality the mare was quite tall at sixteen hands, and he had indeed died by impact, although not from a motorbike and a lamppost. But he had not achieved his target of 320 years. No doubt he would have viewed it as 'two out of three ain't bad'.

His wish was to be cremated to return as quickly as possible to the stardust from which he came. The local crematorium near his birthplace was in line with his wishes of 'completing the circle' and was attended by friends and family. In the waiting area was a plaque mounted on the wall showing this as winner several years running of the "Crematorium of the Year" award. It had always amused him as being so unlikely as an award, and the basis of selection had entertained his vivid imagination when he had been there for a relative's funeral. On that occasion he had been very alive.

Was it based on the efficiency of the ovens, the energy requirements, the speed of service or like hotels the friendliness of the staff, the comfort of the amenities or some other factor unimaginable to ordinary people? Or perhaps just the landscaped grounds with shrubs fertilised by a lot of ash?

Sofia was sure that he would have been thinking along those lines in selecting that location. She also thought he would have imagined the glitzy award ceremony with everyone dressed in black, set off with bright flowery bow ties, or pastel scarves for the ladies, socialising and drinking while the gas barbecue dinner was cooked openly by well-practised staff, and the meat served well done, followed by dancing as the band struck up 'Heaven, I'm in Heaven'… 'Stairway to Paradise', 'Light my Fire' and other equally inappropriate songs.

She remembered that he had once told her about meeting a funeral director who was also a magician. He had imagined him getting confused onstage and producing not a rabbit but something dreadful from a top hat.

The ceremony went well. The good friend who had long ago admired his legs gave a short and light-hearted eulogy suitably irreverent as befitted this situation, and they sang two of his favourite hymns, 'Jerusalem' and 'I Vow to Thee My Country' both of which he had told her he loved from his school days. She hoped he could hear them now, as everyone did their utmost to sing without completely choking on the emotion of the music.

And then slowly they walked past the coffin as his 'play out' music wafted over the speakers, the haunting beauty of 'Oh My Love' which had featured unexpectedly in the film *Drive* and which had never failed to bring a lump to his throat when he played it, and tears from her when he introduced her to it. It was one of their songs, and she was entitled to her tears, partly sadness and partly rejoicing that she had been able to share in his feelings and emotions.

Food was laid on at a local hotel with too much wine, appropriate for such an event, and people reminisced about his life, some shared experiences, and amusing family occurrences. As ever after a funeral, moods turned lighter assisted by the drink but more so by the relief that it was not them left behind in the wooden box. They were aware but wished to avoid acknowledging their own mortality — laughter, alcohol and camaraderie helped prolong their illusion.

She mourned. She knew it would happen, that it would be prolonged, that it would hurt, and that her life for now had been derailed. She also knew that she must go through the necessary steps of grieving. It was a process, a journey she would rather not have had to embark on, but in the end, it would be better, and she would experience some sense of healing. Eventually.

She was aware also that everyone is in mourning throughout their lives. A lost pet as a child, lost loves, lost friends, the death of parents, and of partners. As he had told her, everything is merely on loan for as long as the loan arrangement lasts. But the final repayment inevitably hurts deeply, particularly when unexpected and sudden. Many appear never to recover, and she had often heard of life partners dying within a few days of each other, perhaps grieving so much that they simply lost the will to live on, alone.

She threw herself into more film work, catching up from the time she had excused herself to be with him. His absence after filming was strange and she often started to wake thinking she could feel him next to her, until she woke fully, and the sense of loss flooded back.

Knowing the science of grief was of little consequence when every atom of her mind and body ached for the tenderness and closeness of his touch. Everything reminded her of him. His clothes, photographs, the smell of his aftershave lingering on a shirt in his wardrobe, a pebble collected from a beach on their travels, a pizza recipe, geraniums, a snippet of music... there seemed to be nothing in the universe that did not have some recollection of him for her.

But she survived and eventually healed as much as she would ever achieve, or wish to achieve. She did not wish to fully forget him or his part in her life.

She had spent considerable time preparing herself — make up, jewellery, evening dress... with silk stockings and lingerie — all befitting this anniversary. She spent time looking in the mirror before leaving her cabin for the cocktail reception. She hoped and dared think that she looked beautiful in the long black ballgown she had worn when they first met. The reality was that she looked stunning, and her age added to her allure and attractiveness. He would have told her this and she would have felt his love and admiration from his eyes alone.

He had always thought she had a special beauty and always told her that she outshone every woman in the room.

The party was pleasant, and she dined afterwards with an interesting small group whose conversation was enjoyable. She allowed him to play his usual role of attentive companion, quietly and unobtrusively… and invisibly. In her imagination. For her he was always there beside her.

The sea was calm with a large moon adding to the romance as she walked into the forward piano bar of the Commodore Club. She took a seat at a barstool, elegantly perching on it as he liked, a hint of slim ankle showing above her expensive heels, and the slimness of her body emphasised by the cut of her black ballgown. He liked that people noticed her — men finding her attractive and some ladies often seemingly jealous of her appearance. She liked that he liked it.

She ordered her favourite cocktail to match his star sign and which he had introduced to her those years ago. It came as always in the preposterous drinking vessel shaped like an elephant but with chilled and delicious contents that made it somehow acceptable.

Despite feeling his presence, she had enormous difficulty not crying because he could no longer be there. But she focussed on the happy memories that had started in this place.

As she sipped her drink, she talked with the bar staff, but observed from the corner of her eye the arrival/appearance at the doorway of a tall well-dressed man. She had to admit that he was also strangely good looking in a slightly exotic way that she could not pin down. She found it difficult to distract herself from him but turned her head back to focus on the drink so as not to appear interested. She could not allow that.

She felt her pulse quicken as he slowly approached the bar and stood beside her.

"Excuse me, but are you alone, and would you object to me sitting here?" He gestured to the next bar stool.

"Good evening," she responded playing for some brief thinking time. "In answer to both your questions — No."

She paused briefly watching his reaction. She knew that he would probably have heard that as a rejection and she saw his smile fade slightly. Before he could react further, she spoke again not wishing to be hurtful. "No in the sense that I am not entirely alone on this voyage, my husband is with me, and no that I would not object to you sitting there."

He hesitated and then his smile returned more strongly.

"Thank you, I promise not to bore you and I thought you looked interesting. Is your husband going to be joining you?"

"Bit of a long story," she replied. "Maybe I'll tell you later."

They talked easily and at length and clearly found each other's company enjoyable. Over another cocktail, she explained that her husband had died but that she carried such strong memories and loyalty that he was always with her. His response had been measured and sincere. His situation was that he too had lost a partner he dearly loved and that he carried the memory of her presence with him always. They both thought that life continued in some way after death, as part of the stars or reincarnation of some sort maybe. It was an intellectually matched debate and one from which they both considered that they had learned new viewpoints.

In the small hours she excused herself to retire to bed. They agreed that they might meet up again on the voyage but nothing specific was arranged.

"Probably a silly question," he said as they were preparing to leave, "but have we met before, perhaps on another voyage? There's something very familiar about you."

"I don't know," she answered, "but life sometimes throws people together who get on easily. And yes, I have a not dissimilar feeling somehow."

"Interesting," he said slowly, getting off the bar stool and standing next to her.

He reached slowly into his pocket and produced a small crumpled packet which he held out.

"I really have no idea why I'm asking you this… but would you perhaps like a jellybean?" he asked unexpectedly.